GIRMIT

Stories from the tea gardens of Assam

(Indenture)

GOLAP KHOUND

Translated by
Suranjana Barua

INDIA · SINGAPORE · MALAYSIA

CONTENTS

Translator's Note 5

1. **Girmit** (Indenture) 13

2. **Noyanjulir Jui** (The Fire of Noyanjuli) 28

3. **Sinnomostaar Kothaa** (About a Beheading) 43

4. **Kukur** (Dog) 55

5. **Bandir Bedona** (The Trauma of the Captive) 64

6. **Phoolmoni** (Phoolmoni) 77

7. **Xoti** (Sati) 88

8. **Xindhur Xwad** (The Taste of the Ocean) 101

9. **Eti Mon Jiya Pokhi** (A Heart-Winning Bird) 114

10. **Dhormoghotor Karon Bisari**

   (In Quest for the Reason of the Strike) 126

TRANSLATOR'S NOTE

Golap Chandra Khound's *Girmit* ('Indenture') is a collection of ten short stories based on the tea garden lifestyle of Assam. Khound earned notable fame as a short story writer of the *Ramdhenu* era (1951-1967) – named after the journal *Ramdhenu* which was edited by six illustrious editors including Birendra Kumar Bhattacharya (the first Assamese litterateur to be awarded the Jnanpith). The *Ramdhenu* era is considered to be the golden era of Assamese literature and this well-known journal in Assamese language launched many celebrated writers, novelists, short story writers and critics of Assamese literature such as Bhabendranath Saikia, Lakshminandan Bora, Hiren Gohain, Mamoni Raisom Goswami, Homen Borgohain and many others. *Ramdhenu* marked a new genesis in Assamese literature melding a deep consciousness of Assamese language with contemporary Western philosophy, political awareness and understanding of the human situation. Khound, as a representative of the *Ramdhenu* era, is at his dexterous best in this collection of short stories based on the highly idiosyncratic tea garden way of Assam. The word 'Girmit' roughly translates to 'agreement' or 'contract' and all the stories in this collection feature the indentured labourers and their lives deeply woven with the tea plantation of colonial and post-colonial Assam.

Indentured labour of this region typically had two features – they were transported to plantations over long distances and they were contract bound. It was a double bondage in the sense that the indentured workers could not withdraw their labour in order to bargain over terms of contract or higher wages that led to indentured labour to be viewed as a different form of slavery. The abject penury and the living circumstances often created a vicious cycle of exploitation that resulted in crime, resolution and justice with dire consequences that Khound explores with an almost objective but whimsical language.

Pervading through all his stories in *Girmit* is a deep understanding of Assam, its climate, forests, and of course tea plantations. Khound's language is mystical, exotic, and at the same time foreboding with a deep sense of respect and wariness for the unknown. It creates a deeply unsettling atmosphere bordering on the eerie at times. And the language, although foreboding, is also at the same time esoteric reveling in the bountiful exuberance of Assam's landscape. Moreover, Khound's loquacious prose is interspersed with intense bouts of poetic language making for an enthralling reading but also making its translation a very challenging task. Khound's empathy for the indentured labourers, uprooted from their land and cultures, with their strange language admixed for the British Sahibs but harking back to their own cultures, is manifest in his stories as is his acute awareness of the class consciousness and power dynamics – so much so that the childless couple in 'Kukur' whose dog is mercilessly shot by the Manager as it attacked his expensive pedigreed dog is as helpless as the poverty-stricken 'girmitya' who walk into contracts with the help of the conniving managers in 'Girmit'. Equally lost as the British ('Boga' or fair-skinned) Sahib is the 'Kala' (dark-skinned) Babu who is horrified in 'Sinnamostar Kotha' at the cold blooded beheading of his manager by the natives seeking to avenge the honour of one of their women. *Girmit* has stories of the exploiters and the exploited; of the British Sahibs and their Indian shadows or Babus; of a bountiful landscape and tea garden people; of hopes, horrors and terrifying consequences and of pathos and promise.

The current translation will deeply enrich the available literature of translated literature in Assam. Short summaries of all the 10 stories in Girmit are provided below:

Short Summaries of the Stories in Girmit

Girmit
(*Indenture*)
The titular story *Girmit* on which the collection is ideologically based, revolves around a simple labor girl Mila. Mila's mother had come from Chotnagpur to Assam as a part of a girmit – an agreement –in the hope of living a healthy and wealthy life. But in Assam also their dreams were not fulfilled and they had to face many hurdles. The story mainly centres on Mila who could attract anyone, including the Sahibs, through her beauty but with devastating consequences as young woman was exploited on multiple counts. Her only redemption lay in her own motherhood.

Noyanjulir Jui
(*The Fire of Noyanjuli*)
The esoteric beauty as well as the sinister possibilities hidden in nature as well as human nature find expression in this story. With a deep fascination for the beauty of nature as well as the intriguing hidden depths of human character, the writer weaves the storyline of a river that seems to be on fire at times with that of the General Manager Mr. Thomson whose wild sexual craving for Noyanmoti leads to inexplicable horrors and hauntings. This is the most poetic of the stories in this collection and also one of its most macabre.

Sinnomostaar Kothaa
(About a Beheading)

Sinnomostaar Kothaa (About a Beheading) is a sinister tale of justice as understood by the simple coolies of the tea plantations. Marcus and his wife Maria are tea laborers at Bilobari Tea Estate and they had a reasonably happy married life till the day Gauranga enters into their life. Their lives enmesh into each other and got a horrific ending with Gauranga being beheaded by Marcus on account of the former having an illicit affair with Maria. What is even more terrifying than the horrific muder are the parallels with similar stories being played out at another level between a Babu and a Memsahib under the watchful eyes of the community.

Kukur
(Dog)

Kukur (Dog) is based on a dog named Boli who was the only source of happiness in the life of childless couple Mr. Bora and his wife. After many years of their marriage, this couple was not fortunate to see the face of their own child when one day Boli suddenly entered into their life. But the story takes a tragic turn when Boli is shot by the Manager of Gopalpur Tea Estate – his only fault being that he bit the Manager's pedigreed dog. The shock and the pathos felt by the childless couple, who gave up their dog in the hopes of a promotion, makes for a very gripping narrative with tragic, compassionate undertones to their ambition.

Bondir Bedona
(The Trauma of the Captive)

Bondir Bedona (The Trauma of the Captive) aptly represents power equations. The story is based on the people of Bilobari Tea Estate and 'Phukon Babu' who always spoke against the injustice and domination by the exploiters on the laborers. Therefore, he called all of them to raise their voice against it. But unfortunately, power was not in his hands and he was merely a captive. In return for his true love for the people of this tea garden which made him fight for the welfare of this people, he was served an official notice that asked him to leave the tea garden within sixteen hours. The subtext here is also that he is not the only one captive: so are the hapless workers he wished to liberate with new light and so is Rupa – the married labour girl in love with Phukon.

Phoolmoni
(Phoolmoni)

The story of *Phoolmoni* centres on the life story of Dugaboti and her daughter Phoolmoni. Durgaboti who once lived in Kirtigarh and Phoolmoni came to Assam with her mother as a part of an agreement in the hope of living in peace and satisfaction. But nothing was changed in Assam also as Phoolmoni realized that the evils live everywhere which made their life like hell everywhere.

Xoti
(Sati)

As the title suggests, Sati is the story of a dedicated wife – it provides an in-depth understanding of the life of Lalita who husband is dying but who herself is coveted by the Manager of the Soanjan tea estate. Lalita has given two tight slaps to the Babu on account of his sexual advances – an unheard of incident in the annals of tea garden labourers. Her chastity, strength of character and principles were far more noteworthy than her buxom beauty that men found attractive. The possibilities of her life right after she elopes with her husband Rupnath are contrasted with its start reality when she is reduced to a caregiver of Rupnath whose cough, phlegm and bloodied vomit she regularly has to clean. A woman in the prime of her wife – who having caught the ye of the lecherous manager whom the laborurers had initially taken pride in for being a dark skinned Babu – is doomed to live a life of penury, intensive labour and helplessness. Yet she holds on to hope that one day her dying husband would actually heal revealing an inalienable pathos underlining the lives of tea garden women labourers.

Sindhur Swad

(The Taste of the Ocean)

This story depicts the life, character and circumstances of someone caught in between the laborurers and the British Sahibs – the Chief Medical Officer of the Rupjuli circle Dr. K.M. Dasgupta "M.B.B.S; DTM, MRCP (London)". Ostensibly living the good life in a sprawling bungalow, the forty something Dasgupta has 38 tea estates under his watch. He lives the good life with women for company, has interests apart from medicina and is described as a naturalist, philanderer and world traveler. The story ruminates on the doctor's relationship with Banwari a Saotali whom he had picked up from some organization in central India after she had finished her schooling and completed her nursing training. The story ends with the thoughts engulfing the doctor's mind which flow down as tears which no one would ever know the meaning of.

Eti Mon Jiya Pokhi

(A Heart-Winning Bird)

The most romantic of the short stories in 'Girmit' is *Eti Mon Jiya Pokhi*. A dashing young researcher, Animesh Dutta, from the Department of Anthropology at the university comes with his group for a field trip to the Silguri Tea Estate to study about the Gond tribe who have settled in and around Kaziranga. He meets Champakoli, a young inquisitive tribal girl who introduces her world to her. Champakoli is enamoured by her 'Kaku' and fears the day he will return to the big city – as the story ends, it Animesh who realizes that the time spent with Champakoli as he learns about their society, and that one stolen kiss has meant a lifetime of an experience for him.

Dhormoghotor Karon Bisari
(In Quest for the Reason of the Strike)
The last story of this collection sits at perspectival intersections: a young labourer Gopal had been imprisoned and assaulted by the hired hands of the General Manager Gogoi; and there are counter narratives to this story – of an ongoing strike by the Workers' Association, the police, the unnamed journalist who is also the narrator and the beautiful young woman Radha (who shares Gogoi's bed). The journalist encounters multiple perspectives but seeks the one – Radha's – that possibly links all the other perspectives.

(Dr. Suranjana Barua, Translator)

✳ ✳ ✳

GIRMIT

(INDENTURE)

A lot of people dream.

But what about Mila and others like her?

Indeed, they too have dreams. But these dreams are not the gifts of peaceful sleep or prosperous lives. They dream in reality. Do they have enough leisure time to sleep in beds and have dreams? A single night brings the possibility of a hectic morning for them. Therefore, in reality, with the light of the sun and the blinding rain over their heads, they dream in exchange for each drop of their raw blood.

Mila…

A common girl whose story of birth was an unwritten narrative. Her body was fleshed out in the climes of Assam and the seed that she was had been formed with the confluence of two unexpected forces.

Arjun and Chandraa

Arjun, who had sharpened his intelligence with the tactics of the British Managers of the tea estates of Assam, had entered a worn-out hut of Chotanagpur one fine evening with glittering silver coins. The woman called Chandraa, who was living in that shabby hut with the memories of her late husband, was seen a few days after that along with some twenty people, at a rail station a few miles away.

The land of Assam.

They had heard many tales of golden Assam. Its soil is alluvial and crops grew just like that there. Blessed with the bountiful rains of Ahar and Xawon, people could sow paddy joyfully, all splattered in the mud. How would you like to see the fields during Aghon? As if a golden asol[1] spreads all over the horizon.

And tea plants?

That was also an intriguing thing. Countless trees are planted. Lots and lots of money could be earned just by plucking the leaves. Food was plenty. Blankets were there for winter. Endless leisure time was there over and above the usual amusements, festivals etc. A concrete house to live peacefully. A hospital is also there and a doctor is available in case anybody gets sick. No difficulty, no stress, no crisis…

Assam was a land of gold and a 'heaven on earth' for those whose strength was sucked away by rocky soil, whose nerves become frayed in the sweltering hundred-and-ten-degree summer, and who must pour buckets of the salty sweat of their foreheads to the bosom of the earth to earn just a fistful of grain. They were taken aback when they heard the sound of silver coins – the glitter of which blinds their eyes. They would listen in awe to the tales of this lush green state overflowing with gems and jewels from people who returned from the land of Assam. And, perhaps, they too had dreams of silver coins that glittered.

Chandraa was one amongst them. In the depot, when she was asked if she had any members from her family, she did not answer and absentmindedly kept looking at the sky. Then the *Sardar*[2] of their group, Arjun, came forward and said, "I will be there as her pair."

---

[1] Loose end of saree or sador

[2] Leader/ captain

With this arrangement, Chandraa set foot in the land of Assam on a three-year 'girmit' or agreement. She was counted as a consort of Arjun but since he already had another woman in the tea garden at Assam, she had to live in a separate dwelling.

* * *

The houses allotted to the labourers were better referred to as 'caves' instead of houses. One house with two rooms was fixed for two families. A shed was attached to each room – that was the kitchen. The chicken enclosures and pigsties were close to that. They would sleep in the same room and had their guests over there too. Young girls changed out of their wet clothes after a bath in front of everyone. A young man would sleep with his newly married wife in the presence of his brothers and sisters and parents.

In a corner of this hell, the old drunken father would abuse his children with obscenities and in this place itself, they would give birth to newborn babies. There would be no air circulation and drains would be filled with flies and mosquitoes. The cattle, pigs and hens would render the doorstep filthy. They fell ill – of malaria. Their eyes and faces would become pallid and their bodies would become as if they were fit for cremation. Their stomachs were tormented by hookworms and parasites.

Hospitals were there. They would prescribe and inject quinine. And make them ingest medicines. Some would recover; others would be freed. And in the hope of being born, some would lie on the cot wrapped in a blanket – taking one step at a time towards death. And then, someday, a group of people would be heard wailing loudly and a chapter would end.

Everything would fall silent again. As if complete peace prevailed in all the boundaries of the earth. There was no disturbance anywhere. The garden would keep running at its emotionless pace. The sound of the bell room would convey details about the day's and night's work, as well as intimation regarding leisure time. People would spend each day mixed with laughter and tears while sowing the raw sweat of their foreheads into the soil.

On a rainy day, someday, there would perhaps be heard the sound of *shehnaai* making a lot of noise. What was happening?

A wedding…

Indeed – some twelve-year-old girl would be getting married to a fourteen-year-old boy. The groom likened to Lord Bishnu, would smilingly dance in front of the Babu Sahib's bungalow, dressed in turmeric-laden bright clothes, an umbrella over his head. A group of happy and crazy people would surround him while playing drums and pipes. A dark-skinned plump girl, with stout calves, would move without any hesitation amidst a group of ladies. She was the bride. As per ritual, at the marriage venue, the groom would act as if he was eloping with the girl. That would be the beginning of their conjugal life. Both would sleep on the same bed. Unbeknown to them, they will create their own tiny world. However, unlike the hero and heroine of some romantic novels, they would not have time to measure their love, affection and sympathy for each other. They would not even have time for a honeymoon.

Wasn't it the sole aim of marriage to welcome a new generation? To become a mother and a woman, quite like the fertile cropped area. Only numbers brought them pride – how many children could they birth was their only wish.

This circular form of life was very natural. There was nothing to be surprised about. Birth, death, marriage and union – these were very simple things to ponder over.

Still, beauty resides in the motion of these motions. Waves of silvery light create dreams of illusions. Waves over waves would flow over the dunes of the heart to the pleasant rhythms of beauty's dance… If one was to wake up in the middle of the night and listen to the sounds of the leaves of the tree glistening in the light of the pale-yellow moon in the sky, one would hear, with just a little more effort, amidst the leaves of the tea shrubs, *shirish* and *gulmohar,* the sound of the *madol* being played far away in the lines, getting lost in the deep calm silence of the night…

They would have delicious homemade liquor and dance *jhumoor* in the moonlight under the clear skies to remove their fatigue. Many men. Many women. Many lives. They did not have any demands on the body. They are not attracted towards any particular part of the women's bodies. There was no grief, no inertia. They only had happiness engulfing their bodies and souls and spreading to their very existence. They would fall asleep in the courtyard or entrance of their houses while singing songs and dancing. The pale moon will gradually disappear into the horizon while watching them.

A night would end and there would be the beginning of a new dawn. The leaves of the *shirish* and the *gulmohar* would tremble in the chilly wind of the morning. Far away could be heard the cacophony of a flock of birds at the crack of dawn. People are waking up. The light coming in from the eastern gateway of the horizon brought with it a busy day – a green collection of 'two leaves and a bud'. This was their unwritten history.

* * *

In one of the leaves of this very history were the names of Chandraa and Arjun. And it was from the seed of this Arjun that Mila was conceived in the womb of Chandraa. And then one day, her tiny little body was born in the land of Assam.

Chandraa had lost her trust in Arjun that day itself when she could perceive the difference between the real scenario of the tea gardens of Assam and what was explained in his speeches. But there was no way out – the first problem was that she was a 'girmitiya' by agreement.

And the other was that she was a woman.

And therefore, against her wishes and despite her hatred towards Arjun, she had to surrender the deepest recesses of her body to the octopus-like influence of Arjun.

A girl child was born amidst the dirt and grime of the tea garden.

Her name was Mila.

Eighteen years thus passed by in everyday routine. The rest would also have passed by with nothing remarkable happening if Mr. Jefferson had not set foot in the soil of Assam flying in on a huge sky master of B.A.O.C and if I had not joined as a doctor in the garden.

No – a story was born. And it is the story of a civilized nation that I want to write about.

✳ ✳ ✳

Jefferson.

He might have heard about the tea gardens of East India while roaming around after the completion of the primary course of his Engineering degree and after having registered his name in the Employment Exchange office.

India.

The land of witchcraft and mystery.

There was an opportunity to work in the tea gardens of Assam. One had to be there companionless although there was money there and people could spend their lives in great comfort and pleasure. Relatively, one would not feel the pressure of responsibility. One could relish the pleasure of having no companions.

With this hope, one day, he flew across the seas and came over.

Mr. Jefferson was the young Assistant Manager and he had already spent two months in the garden.

One day… a day that brought in the reprimand of destiny.

The raw green leaves that had been plucked were being weighed in the afternoon. *Chota Sahib* i.e., Assistant Manager, Mr. Jefferson, was supervising the work nearby. One by one, the women were placing their baskets on the balance, showing the weight and passing them on. Suddenly, he noticed a healthy girl with bright eyes and an oval face put her basket on the spring balance. Some buttons of her blouse which had come loose could be seen through her cheap colourful saree as she held her hands upwards.

A violent breeze of the forests coursed through his heart. Jefferson gulped and asked her name.

Her name was Mila.

She then left the spot taking with her that beauteous body.

She was a pretty girl. I had seen her many times. One day, she came to sweep my house and rub it with clay. Even though she was the daughter of a labourer, she was neatly dressed and dignified in her speech which is why I liked her. My little children also liked her and she used to address my wife as Baideo[3].

Gradually, a loving tie was forged between my family and her. One day I jokingly asked her, "Hey Mila, won't you do a marriage?"

---

[3] Assamese term of address for elder sister or senior woman

She did not say anything but smiled instead. Some two years ago, it seems a young man had taken her mother's consent and had taken her away after giving her some money and clothes. But the man was very rowdy and a drunkard and they frequently got into fights. Hence, Mila returned to her mother's home out of her own choice. Now, she was earning her living.

Her body shone with good health and she had dimples in her plump cheeks when she smiled. When one saw her smile, one felt like seeing it again – her teeth were also clean and symmetric.

Such was Mila. It is sufficient for a young healthy girl like her to create an illusion in the heart of a lustful man with a small smile and a gentle trembling of the ample portions of her figure.

Jefferson all but melted for her. He would ask people about her: "*Bohot accha chokri*" ("Very good girl.")

He offered rewards to his bearers and asked them to bring her to his bungalow.

The people of the garden started talking about Mr. Jefferson saying that he usually went to the garden in search of Mila amidst all the other girls. He always found some opportunity to talk to her in broken Hindi.

"Come to my bungalow, you will get lots of baksheesh[4]."

She could understand his covert gestures but never said anything. She smiled but she understood. The *Sahib* came forward to talk leaning on her body. Mila only laughed. Sunlight fell on her body which she had bathed after oiling with mustard oil. Salty sweat was flowing down the dimples of her cheeks which he wished to touch with his lips. Her blouse was short and the naval was showing. It was like a small pit. Her bosom seemed a bit listless as if they were turned downwards.

---

[4] Tips

Jefferson salivated – his heart trembled and he felt as if his insides had turned dry. A disobedient lust had trampled on an obedient mind and squished it away.

But the clever girl did not give him any chance. Still, could anyone tie an unruly elephant full of unfulfilled desires with a few strands?

And therefore, the incident happened.

❊ ❊ ❊

Within moments, the news spread like wildfire. But nothing untoward happened on account of the crafty *Sardar* and simple-hearted accountant. Jefferson confessed his fault and agreed to give her a baksheesh of Rs. 10. She kept quiet. What was the use of quarrelling with the British *Sahib?*

The manager also got to know about this unofficially. He was an English gentleman. An experienced and responsible person, he was very considerate as well as mature. Therefore, he warned Jefferson who seemed about to hit the feet of morality itself with an axe.

"I might not be your superior, Mr. Jefferson! But see, you are an English man, you hail from a dignified society, no–?"

Indeed, Jefferson was the representative of a civilized society.

And Mila was a common labour girl. She had not been refined by modern education and tastes. She could not easily untie the knot of superficiality.

A section of the society, perceiving this weak base in them, thought that their individuality and their self-respect could be bought by tempting them with money and bribes. Just because these people had certain limitations in terms of love, hatred or self-respect, would the people from the high strata of society slacken at their own pace?

Jefferson became shrewd and even more stubborn. He wanted to enjoy Mila by any means. She was like the proverbial golden apple.

There was a thunder of the unfulfilled desires in the heart of the young man sleeping alone, companionless, in a spacious room of a deserted bungalow. Each drop of blood was simmering in unrestrained lust. It was as if he had to overpower her in this bed itself… or in any other place in the world… this girl, whom he had seen after arriving in this tea garden that seemed like a forest. He felt like biting and squishing her attractive body which lay hidden under her common clothes. On this bed or in any corner of the world. In the sanctity of the darkness, the demon in Jefferson's mind came alive.

The octopus!

It was easy for the flower to get entangled in coils. Even the octopus knew that. It was but natural. Hence Jefferson applied a tactic – he would not approach the flower and he would not reach out to the flower. There might be snakes lurking.

The crafty attraction would bring a bunch of lovely colourful flowers and place them by the bedside for the pleasure of the creator. No one would know. There would be no problem. Satiation would herself hold your hand out of her own will – you just had to accept it.

Preparations started for that and the python shed its skin.

Mila too was a flower.

And one day, entrapped by attraction, she also got lured. The eyes of the python in disguise burnt bright and the petals of the flower began to fall against its harsh pressure. They withered and felt the pain too but then attraction was crafty. I also got the hint of Mila's unfortunate surrender as I am a doctor.

How?

I am unable to express in this story – how? Jefferson called me aside and implored. He had doubts in his eyes.

"Doctor, very unfortunate! She is a very inexperienced girl and got a very bad haemorrhage. Please, Doctor! Take note of my respect – I hope she will be alright."

A very pale, tired girl… extreme pain expressed through her eyes and face. She was quiet.

I noticed that she had difficulty walking.

Animal! I could only think of this word after seeing her. But Mila did not get freedom. The mute hunted went to the hunter of its own will and against the pressure of the evil machine, the soft soil gave way and was lost.

Days passed by thus.

She started visiting the hospital at times. Her desolate unorganized life made her anxious and her eyes reflected her fatigue. She started feeling dizzy and would vomit while working in the garden.

People started to talk about how she had conceived on account of *Chot Sahib*[5] (Jefferson) and this assumption became clearer day by day. And one day…

An incident happened.

The young man she had been married to may have been instigated by a few people and he came forward for a fight. He got a huge gathering, drunk on rice beer, incited them to anger and they gathered in front of the office with large knives and sticks in their hands. Each one of them was using abusive terms and swear words.

"Bring out the Chot Sahib… that mother*** and sister***. You scoundrel… come out!"

The manager was not there in the office. Jefferson was inside the factory and there was uproar outside. Someone said, "Let's go to the Bara Sahib's bungalow."

This outburst was not completely unexpected.

---

[5] Abridged for Chota (young) Sahib

While working in the garden, Mila fainted that day and a few people carried her to the hospital. She regained consciousness in the evening.

She never knew, while lying on the sick bed at the hospital, that her once husband had gone to the Manager with the intent to create trouble.

As destiny would have it, Mila's labour pain started that day itself.

I got up at the crack of dawn on hearing the nurse's calls. I was being called as Mila had again fainted at night and was moaning.

I reached the hospital and saw that the patient was unconscious. At my indication, the nurse removed her clothes all the way up. That entire area was full of blood and her face was contorted in pain. Her beautiful fleshy body had become disgusting to look at.

The nurse was holding her in a pose that would induce labour. A svelte young girl with little experience... a portion of the newly born came in contact with the air of the earth... Slowly...

Mila moaned again but the nurse did not give her any chance to bring her two knees closer.

Slowly... Slowly.

"You are a mother! You will have to keep patience! Slowly... slowly... These difficult moments would go away like this..."

It is as if the last red ink has just come out with a natural sound and flowed over the ground...

✳ ✳ ✳

A healthy reddish complexioned baby boy took shelter on mother earth. His hair was red. He had western features in his eyes, face and structure. Mila became the mother of this child and – perhaps – Mr. Jefferson was the father.

And therefore, the labourers in the garden got agitated.

Mila's reputation had been ruined. As had the labourers'. The people were surprised and perturbed.

Jefferson Sahib was not there in the garden. He had taken leave and had supposedly gone off to Shillong.

The child remained in Mila's custody. Even though she never wanted to bear the seed of the foreign Sahib, when that tiny seedling split out of her body and came to this world in a new form with a cry, it was as if all the guilt had been removed from her heart. In just that moment when the newborn baby came to her and a mild cry was heard, her vulnerability was gone. Even though it was unwanted, she could not deny this donation. It was God's girmit.

Slowly the clothes over her breasts were removed and she could feel that very tender warm lips had pressed over her breasts tightly. With every gulp, she could feel an ethereal thrill in her body.

The manager was able to calm the people. If the incident was true, then Mila would get a good amount of money. Her ex-husband claimed that he should get the money instead. The manager replied it would be decided by the *Panchayat*.

They returned. And the flow of discontent abated.

And one day, Mila was released from the hospital with a baby in her lap.

The wheels of time moved on.

* * *

Sands and dust, pearls and gems all became history in one of the pathways left behind. The restless waves of the mind slowly settled down. And regularity returned to the heart of the garden. The toll of the bell gave intimation of the morning, afternoon and evening work and leisure.

The madol[6] would play in the evening

In the middle of the colony, somebody would scold any invisible enemy after having had local liquor. Dogs barked. Normal pace returned to Mila's life too.

But *Chota Sahib* never returned. Jefferson. But he left behind proof of his illegal desires. A part of Jefferson who was born from Mila's womb… an innocent human child. In the flickering light of the kerosene lamp, Mila cooks food in an untidy hut. Nearby, her baby lying in a sack starts to cry and Mila runs to pick him up in her lap. And she would insert one of her nipples into his mouth.

Arjun had driven away Chandraa and now both the mother and daughter stayed together.

Chandraa was part of a three years girmit. It was over but she never returned to her own state. It is the beginning of a never-ending agreement. Their dreams were broken long back. The golden seeds which they imagined had not grown in the alluvial land of Assam. Nor could they gather precious gems and jewels. They could not save silvery coins either.

The owners of tea industries might take pride in the fact that they tried not to give less than the minimum required money which would enable the labourers to live a low-cost life.

One day…

During the ceaseless rain of Ahar, a woman came to our house.

My daughter recognized her and shouted: "Mila! Mila!"

"*Babu*…," she smiled.

I felt good to see her kind and affectionate smile. Her old charm had not faded yet. She was pure. She was washed with

---

[6] A musical instrument (wooden drum)

fire. Her motherhood, which she could feel in her heart, had washed away all her guilty. She was clean now.

I stroked the head of that mother who was standing in her wet clothes and lovingly asked her: "So, Mila, how are you?"

✳ ✳ ✳

Noyanjulir Jui

(THE FIRE OF NOYANJULI)

Noyanjuli!

The living dream of a dead source in the identity-less horizon afar – Noyanjuli aka Noyanjuri was a symphony of waves flowing below bushes of *karxola, bon birina* and *garmani.* Its history had been created in the heart of some silent century of the past with the songs of its soil and dust; with the anguish of the blue skies scratched by the cries of the thirsty bird and the thieving hawk; and the wails of the dead cemetery. Who was there today to give the tidings of this nectared history?

Still, the split ikora[7], torahabi, bonkosu[8] and dhekiya[9] or the footprints of the people and the dried peel of the betel nuts might tell you that Noyanjuli is alive. Noyanjuli's dreams had not died. Those songs were the songs of life that were alive.

Those songs were the songs of golden dreams and laughter and tears.

Even today, when dark, dense clouds thunder during the new rains, when the rhythm of the clouds dance unencumbered in the *ahot*[10]*, sotiyon and the ejar*[11], then, Noyanjuli turns young again. It becomes young in that glimmering youth. The arrogant Noyanjuli's powerful waves dash against the *birina* and the *tora* bushes flattening these and making them slumber.

---

[7] Ravenna grass
[8] Wild taro
[9] Vegetable fern
[10] Peepal
[11] Giant crape myrtle

The crazed gait of a mountain maiden comes over Noyanjuli then.

If you wish, you too keep going upstream through Noyanjuli…

And then wait a while.

And then, with the gratification and the silence of the pure leaves, put your ear to it and listen to your core. Somebody is crying! Someone was hiding and crying now and then in that unpeopled silence… in that deserted place.

Whose voice was this?

Was it some woman? Or some supernatural entity?

Far from the skies, in a space not easily touchable by the din of the rabble, in this companionless silence of the core of the forest, who was it that was whimpering? Which woman's cry of her anguished heart had made you static by the banks of Noyanjuli?

Who knows? Maybe that was the cry of silence.

Or maybe it was the cry of birth of the mortal emptiness. There was no rest to this whimpering. Till the time there is a future, till the time the *tora* jungle shed tears by the banks of the Noyanjuli in the rains, there was no end to this mysterious story. Till then, there would be no end to the whimpering.

I had gone to see Noyanjuli. Noyanjuli was a fragrant poem touched by the rhythm of the depth of intensity. In the nectarine moment in which I had been present there – guarding it on both sides, standing satisfied in the middle of the awed forest, was a dejected evening. On the far horizon, the crimson beams of the fading sun had created an impeccable scene against the backdrop of the sky-piercing clouds. There was such a mystique of loneliness over the ground.

That Noyanjuli and that symbol of the intangible flames of the heart… the history of its birth was fiery. I thank the one from whose mouth I had heard this story. It was he who had shown me this fire in the heart of Noyanjuli.

The fire of Noyanjuli!

Perhaps this fiery history was all that Noyanjuli had.

Who was it that had said there was an evil spirit here? Everyone became different here. Many people would go out of their homes having heard the beckoning of the wordless night and would go ahead on a path of no return. There were still a lot of people at Noyanjuli who could give a clear description of who these people were; when, how and what exactly had happened. But then these are useless things for now.

But you see, these are true things. You can write all of these. But then do people have the leisure to hear the truth? I have seen many people spending days or weeks seeking the mercy of the goddess or the blessings of the gods they create. And yet, they did not have a moment for the one who created the gods. He had said.

I thought about it – it was my duty to write the truth about these people who had been burnt by Nayanjuli's fire. Else it would be a crime.

But then, would the fact about the heart-breaking cry that was heard time and again in the unpeople jungle, stay unexpressed forever? Then why was it that the bricks of the dead cemetery had still kept alive the epitaph of the horrific story of the past? Then why was it that the living dreams of so many people had become traceless by the accursed fire of Noyamtori?

All things cannot be started at once. Hence, whenever you go upstream via Noyanjuli; stand below that ancient banyan and see the broken bricks strewn around an old grave, it would be good to take that violent story as our primaeval story.

And maybe those very things would become murderous Noyanjuli's story. Surely, those were very old stories- there are no historical witnesses there apart from the broken grave.

A deserted place can be called by any other name quite well because this name is not there from the beginning; rather, it is called deserted only after it becomes so. Similarly, Noyanjuli's name was not always so – a place is called *'juli'* only after it becomes an evil accursed spirit; where someone's wails are heard into the night and where people go out in the middle of the night.

One such person who had gone out never to come back was the late Mr. Thomson. It is from him only that I came to know of one such person who had gone out never to come back: the late Mr. Thomson.

No one is curious to know even today what was the earlier name of Noyanjuli. What is the need to know the name of a densely wooded place, lying outside the purview of the civilized world's gives and takes, about seventy-five to eighty years ago?

If you can, with a little bit of patience, do some research, you will be able to find out that the grave belongs to Mr. Thomson. They say it takes a lot of tears to create a grave – they say it takes a lot of prayers for the soul of a dead person to find peace in heaven. It is perhaps, after all, the efforts of humans regarding a person's death, that the world seems morose.

But the grave that had been made of the bricks lying under the ancient banyan by the banks of the Noyanjuli came into existence due to an urgent need. There had been not a single drop of tear for that or any prayers. Maybe even the surprised God forgot about that death.

"What had made that grave necessary?" I asked.

Removing the spectacles that age had gifted him with, he said: these things are hearsay. After all, it was a long while ago.

This means, even before people on the side of law got wind of the matter, the General Manager's head and torso were buried there. After that, they collected a few bricks and created a grave over that place.

General Manager Mr. Thomson had gone out, never to return. There was no discernible cause for his disappearance. Because even before there could be any information, the red-haired head in one place and the torso with the congealed brackish blood that had been lying under the ancient banyan were seen to belong to Mr. Thomson.

In other words, Mr. Thomson had been murdered.

About six or seven years before this incident, a hard-working British youth had reached that place with truckloads of things. It came to be known later that he was Mr. Thomson. An engineer, some craftsmen and a few families of labourers belonging to hilly areas of Central India had come with Mr. Thomson.

There was no special history and neither had there been any human settlement in that place where they had reached by truck which had traversed four hours at the rate of twenty miles per hour, after journeying from a special railway station in Assam. It was not that the sun had not given light or there had been no rains in that place, infested with innumerable pythons, wolves and deer.

And that is why Mr. Thomson had arrived in that heavily woody place for timber business. He aimed to establish a sawmill there and earn silver money in Assam's jungles.

The Eastern Saw Mills.

General Manager Mr. Thomson. A new colony sprung up around that factory. Labourers' huts came up and cemented houses for craftsmen, clerks and overseers came up. Houses with lawns came up for the Sahibs. There would be many a siren in the mornings and evenings. The smoke from the chimneys of Eastern Assam Saw Mills could be seen from afar slowly assimilating in the wind.

They got habituated to another thing in addition to the siren – 'they' implies the labourers.

"Your souls will be at peace. Pray to Jesus – Jesus will relieve you of your ailments."

The ambrosial words of Jesus wafted through the jungles of Assam. There was a significant prevalence of malaria in that place with a humid environment, infested with mosquitoes. People would get fever and become weak. Some would have their ribs sticking out; eyes sunken in hollows and tummies bloated like a bamboo casket.

When there was a big spreading of this disease, the assistant of the mill – Brown – would go out in the morning in his car and come back late at night. The next morning, a man in a long white hanging coat with a big moustache and beard, with a smile across his face, would be seen standing by the patients. He would feed them something and then say:

"Pray to Jesus. Jesus will relieve you of your ailments."

It cannot be said if they prayed to Jesus but the people did not die. The smoke from the chimneys of Eastern Assam Saw Mills would keep emanating regularly.

The owner of the sawmill Mr. Thomson went out of his home one day to never return. He had told me once in the context of the conversation: "You know; this has nothing to do with ghosts or spirits. This is about human beings. There were ghosts earlier. I had heard in my childhood once a friend of my uncle had gone to the forest for some wood and he had seen an eight-foot-tall demon in broad daylight. But I do not believe in ghosts nowadays. You also do not believe."

The story of the ghost was this:

✳ ✳ ✳

Many days ago, an unknown terror took the form of a bodiless soul and roamed about amidst the night's darkness and the jungle's solitude. The night watchman of the sawmill has seen a few people roaming about suspiciously, in the moonlight piercing through the forest. Who knew – maybe some unseen sign had beckoned to General Manager Mr. Thomson. That was the death invitation in Noyanmoti's story.

This happened about eight months ago.

Mr. Thomson who had gone out fishing one afternoon saw a woman bathing in a mountain stream and then changing her clothes. He hesitated to go forward. Suddenly the woman shuddered and took a few steps towards the bank. She touched her underbelly with her right hand to determine something and then she lifted the blue saree that she was wearing bottom up. Mr. Thomson was staring at the scene.

Her clothes went up beyond her knees revealing a portion of her thigh – embarrassed, Thomson turned his face away.

"Ahh!"

Thomson was startled to hear a sudden cry. He saw that she had fallen on the ground – her clothes were bloodied and her hands were red. Thomson ran towards her. The young woman had a huge mountain leech stuck in the palm of her right hand. It must have stuck to her while she was bathing and, finding a chance near her thigh, had started sucking blood. When she removed it, the place where its mouth had been started gushing blood. The clothes that she was wearing turned red.

With the agility of an experienced person, Mr. Thomson picked her up and then smeared a bit of the sticky soil from the river in the area. The woman had not lost consciousness.

It is here that Noyanmoti's story begins.

No one keeps track of how this story had been born under the cloudless skies of some silent past. But it can be gleaned that there was the unending appeal of raw blood and flesh at the base of this story.

And that is why, unbeknownst to many, a woman had disappeared from the Eastern Saw Mill colony one day. And, pretty soon, it was clear as day that this woman was Noyanmoti.

There was a stir amongst the labourers – the widowed mother of Noyanmoti went mad. The place was abuzz with all kinds of stories – but there was only one question that hit everyone to the core: where had Noyanmoti disappeared? What had happened to her?

One day, a group of people went to the General Manager. They had heard murmurs for a while now that Noyanmoti used to receive a commission from the Sahib even though she did not work at the mill. No one got to know on what account and taking advantage of which situation the General Manager had acted out this despicable drama.

Be that as it may, these people went and presented themselves in the courtyard of the General Manager, when Thomson was not at home. With dramatic seriousness, the priest had come outside wearing a cloak.

"All of you, be at peace. Be at peace."

They had not come in search of peace. They had come looking for news about Noyanmoti.

They told the story of Noyanmoti's disappearance and were getting ready to tell more. But instead, they all hung their heads and froze like stone sculptures in the face of that majestic and vast personality.

Any unusual event turns usual with time. The iron wheels of the chariot of time flatten out puddles and potholes. Similarly, the heat of Noyanmoti's story abated in time but the story gave birth to severe trauma. Taking advantage of the night's darkness, bodyless terrors started roaming along the sides of the Eastern Saw Mills. With the dust of suspicion and the garb of mystery, an unknown evil spirit walked with powerful steps, creating new wonders.

I wanted to find out if Thomson was a human or an animal. As far as I know, he had never imagined that I would ask him such a question. And hence he gave a meaningless laugh and said: "Yes, that is also something to mull over."

And yet, I thought about it as I started to write the story – there were two Mr. Thomsons: one who had established the Eastern Saw Mills, was an expert in business, hard-working and a citizen of a civilized nation. And the other was the evil representative of a primitive man holding despicable thoughts, crazy for the living soil and fleshy body of the main summer regions of Assam.

The feelings of Mr. Thomson degraded under the influence of alcohol and the company of beauteous women, had taken an oath the day they had encountered the lush, svelte, and variegated body of Noyanmoti that they would bite and tear off each portion of that soft body. The two eyes of Thomson had gleamed with the horrific influence of a long hungry spirit.

Let it be – this is not a novel that would necessitate the creation of a utopia by keeping the reader enthralled through the touch of magical characterizations. This Mahabharat regarding Thomson is not something I need to prove. So let me summarize the things regarding Noyamoti.

✳ ✳ ✳

Noyanmoti was a woman.

Since the dark ages, the truths that had been engrained for women, regarding a woman's body and mind, like some restless meteor, had been running uninterrupted into the modern ages and were now standing at the threshold of this age, and these held true for Noyanmoti too. And perhaps there had been no need to turn the pages of life's manuscript in search of a context. Whatever you have in your hand is the reality – whatever you see in front of yourself in the incontrovertible truth.

Whatever the decision was had to be done. Then the option was that whatever was doable, was also proved to be the decision. And the question was, what had made the doable the necessary? What was the need? Which illiterate would utter the word 'justice' in this forest, far away from the civilized world where the sun pours its damp light? No one in the vicinity of the Eastern Saw Mill had the leisure to discuss and debate things with specific words like 'justice' and 'injustice.'

And Noyanmoti's? Pah!

Whether she was a human or something wild, it was understood naturally enough that there were few things real and others were functional. She had understood what Thomson was.

Where were the pupils of Thomson's eyes hovering around? What hand had his powerful hirsute hand dealt? Where on her body, had the face and teeth of Thomson, who smelt like a tiger, bitten and held?

Wasn't there any relevance to all this? Noyanmoti was different in build as compared to the other women of the colony, in that swampy region which was reigned over undisputedly by banyan and bamboo and where the serpent and wild animals caused terror. Amongst the women above twenty, who had drunk and breathed the crazed air and water of this magical land and who dragged the sawdust from the sawmills to throw far away, Noyanmoti was distinctive. Having never tasted the saltiness of life's complicated ocean, her mind was the green meadow of the Tundra region.

The cunning guileful Thomson got a whiff of that virgin green meadow. For the British businessman who singlehandedly established the Eastern Assam Saw Mill, would money, chicken, goats, deer, gin and whisky suffice?

Hence the sawmill and the settlement in contact with it fell into the bind of an old cycle and started moving around in its limited path. Bodiless terrors took advantage of the night and started roaming around with steps. The python of darkness kept climbing with a creak.

Maybe some unseen gesture had beckoned to General Manager Thomson.

Sometimes, the dried bamboo of the hills rub against each other and get set on fire. There is no one to extinguish it. On the blazing days of Phagun, the fire is re-enacted in the jungles. How was one to draw water from the river and calm the flickering tip? When the inhuman trust-breaking ember set the anger and self-consciousness of the barbaric tribes of Central India on fire, that fire does not get satiated without the living sacrifice of retribution. It cannot be done.

At such times, the trademark message of peace from the beak of that priest was like a drop of dew on a blade of grass in front of that crazed fire.

Tradition had kept the Indian mind dominated by white skin. That tradition was the acceptance of the simplicity of cunning. This tradition was the structural cowardice of regional or communal weakness in the face of a powerful personality. Of the force of habit. That is why they had indeed calmed down when the cultured and calm priest asked them to calm down when a group of them had suddenly turned up at General Manager Thomson's residence, asking the reason for Noyanmoti's disappearance. They kept standing there in silence for a long while; one or two of them murmured something and then, they all turned back home.

But had the fire in their hearts been extinguished?

No one had asked for this news and no one had given it. But one fine day, like the powerful action of a drama, this closed door had been thrown open: when Mr. Thomson's night watchman shrieked loudly and fell unconscious. What? What an accident!

People nearby saw a primaeval wonder. Terror. Indeed, it was a terror. Far away from the civilized world, if amidst this forest surrounded by four-legged violence, someone saw early in the morning right in the middle of the courtyard, some bamboo vessels for husking paddy, vermilion, a cock with its throat slit open, a few strands of hair and some coagulated blood in an earthen pot, then was there any reason not to be afraid?

Mr. Thomson hurried out – his eyes still bore traces of suddenly disrupted sleep. The people looked at him. But…

But all this? What? What was all this?

The pupils in the eyes of the people were still by then as if they were the pupils of the dead. Their lips were silent. Static. Perhaps the thought of impending trouble had created a furore in their hearts.

They say that someone had smeared blood on the clothes that the Manager was wearing. What a strange thing!

What a conspiracy!

The sun was yet to wake up – there was still almost an hour for the factory bell to ring. There was nothing. The wind was static. Calm. But which bodiless terror had strewn the ashes of some ancient dark age that they were all so silent! There was not a word uttered by anyone.

Mr. Thomson screamed. "Who? Who has done this deed? You have committed murder. You have done voodoo. Voodoo!" and he screamed again. "Tell me who did this!"

Who would say which man had done it? Someone found out – which evil person's wild conspiracy had smeared raw blood on Thomson's clothes or who had given birth to a live fear in the courtyard of the bungalow with these primitive necromantic things?

Was this the conspiracy of the bodiless ghost of Noyanmoti?

Who knew? Who would say? The twentieth century's science was non-functional here. It was maimed.

General Manager Mr. Thomson went mad.

Unrest, misfortune and terror took birth in the Eastern Assam Saw Mill. Time went back many thousands of years.

Someone whimpered scarily every night in the woods afar. The wind would drag in someone's long cries through the darkness. The darkness grew even denser. The nights grew even more suspicious. The fears dug in even deeper and set up base.

Who was to say what kind of inevitability was being created?

Mr. Thomson grew agitated. The sleep in his eyes took flight. Death came on tiptoe speedily. The shimmer of life's glitter was killed off in the shadows of the fearful hand of horrible and conniving death step by step. It was as if the bed had been lit with the fire of a funeral pyre. Restless, Mr. Thomson went out…

The night was a terrible hell.

The darkness was a blood-sucking demon.

Death came on tiptoe step by step. It could jump on you at any moment like a violent animal. Its sharp claws could strangle you. It could bite your neck with teeth that tore into flesh.

The sawmill was standing far off. On the other side of it was a forested mystery. Thomson kept staring at it in complete self-oblivion. A nightmare!

The wind wailed.

Silence cried. The world with which people were familiar was slowly reducing. Perhaps it ended up in an identity-less dot. On the other hand, the world that people were not familiar with grew bigger and turned into a nebula which could not be gazed upon by the human eye or perceived by the human mind.

Unconsciously, Thomson's legs took him forward.

The inevitability that had created the mystery – the history of death.

It seems a lot of vultures were soaring in the skies. One or two of them noticed. The people were roaming around at that time.

In other words, the Manager was lost.

Everything was quite normal at night – informed the people at the bungalow. There was nothing untoward. But the Sahib did not wake up in the morning. This means, there was no one in the bed. Then where had Thomson gone?

Assistant Manager Brown felt his European blood boil up. Thomson had to be found.

The factory siren went off as if possessed… Aaaaaa! Aaaaaaa!

The people started gathering – workers, officials everybody… Brown was pacing around like boiling water.

"Take a count! How many men are there? Take a count!"

The people were lined up and counted. Three men and one woman were missing.

✳ ✳ ✳

He stopped after telling the detailed story. He removed his spectacles, kept them on the table and took a few deep breaths.

"You know, we are listening to all these stories as if they are fairy tales. Are we police or investigators who would peck and prove what is true and what is false? Alright – let us have a cup of tea now. what do you say?"

He finished the rest of the story with the cup of smoked tea in his hands – how Mr. Brown engaged people and looked up every leaf in the jungle; how a few people followed the activities of the vultures and finally found Thomson hacked into two; how he laid laws to rest beneath the tree; how those missing people were never found…

A lot of people had seen a figure wrapped in white clothes roaming by the river after that. In due course, people started a rumour that it was the ghost of Noyanmoti who had disappeared and died suddenly.

As days passed by, people started calling the river Noyanjuri. But no one could give the correct information as to when Noyanjuri became Noyanjuli.

SINNOMOSTAAR KOTHAA

(ABOUT A BEHEADING)

During the rule of Khalifa Harun-al-Rashid, a common man had been able to sit on the throne of Baghdad for a day. A Sultan for one day.

There is nothing to be surprised about here. But coming back home after five years, when I heard that Abola has become *Memsahib* now, like ten other common people, I, who had done research on sugarcane and earned a doctorate, was also surprised.

Abola Kalita was the only daughter of Sundar Kalita, an Assistant Teacher at our local school. She took admission in Intermediate Arts here after having passed matriculation in the second division. She learnt to dress well and according to some keen observers, the superficial seriousness of some baroness from the Middle Ages was reflected in her gait.

Ms. Kalita became Mrs. Chaliha when she married Bijoy Chaliha. There is no use in introducing Mr. Chaliha, who started speaking in a foreign accent soon after high school. At present, he is the Assistant Manager of Bilobari Tea Estate. Isn't this enough by way of his introduction?

It was as per his invitation that I arrived at a small station. The driver of *Chot Sahib* paid me a grand salute after considering that a well-dressed I, surely had to be the guest of *Chot Sahib.* (Many critics say that the British officers had taught their coolies very well, how to pay obeisance to them by bending their heads and waist.)

The land master of Bijoy Chaliha started moving through the rows of tea, shirish and medeluwa trees. The Bilobari Tea Estate was sitting with bundles of money against the background of the hills far away.

From the other side of the bamboo grove, engulfed with the sounds of countless cranes, the sun was playing hide-and-seek with the plants and trees on this side. Slowly, the car stopped beside the portico of the huge bungalow of Bijoy Chaliha. Just then, I saw a handsome young man and a beautiful young woman far away. Bijoy and Abola. I wanted to look at Abola again since I had not seen her in five years, when Bijoy shouted, "Hey scientist! Why are you not getting down?" The driver opened the door and respectfully stood there. Fastening the button of my coat, I got down.

Surrounded by the mystery of the deeps between the hills and the forest, perhaps, dusk descended sooner on the Bilobari Tea Estate. The bungalow of Assistant Manager Bijoy Chaliha was lit with electric lights. The cries of the foxes were far away and, nearer to the flower garden, the chorus of the grasshoppers could be heard. The officers' bungalows stood as symbols of pride and prosperity in a deserted area devoid of population. As if, there was always a respectful distance between them and the common people.

I was looking at the oil paintings while lying on the bed. A girl opened the door and stood there. With a lot of hesitation and uncertainty, she said, "Huzoor, the *Memsahib* calls for you."

"*Memsahib?* Oh, Abola!" I corrected my mind. The girl left and in her place there stood Abola Chaliha with a bright and fair forehead; a proud and serious demeanour, clad in a white dress.

"You…I mean… I did not wake you up since you were sleeping." She stood near my bed with a smile.

"Pah! What are you muttering? Please come and sit." As if I was in hurry to see the time, I pulled her left hand closer to me.

"Isn't it time for your Sahib to arrive yet?" I asked.

"He already came. He will not go anywhere now. He goes to the club on Sundays otherwise he breaks soda bottles to read novels. Come on – get up."

This was Abola. I still have not less than twenty love letters from her in my box. All that was in the past now. Now she is a Memsahib. Well, there is no need of writing a letter enumerating all that I did while visiting Bijoy Chaliha's place. But, if I do not express the story that my modern mind took faith in, then it will be an injustice to Rupali.

However, Rupali can't be the heroine of any play. If she gets recognized in people's judgement and if she does not become the second edition of her mother, then I will be happy and she will get some peace in that hellhole. I had been stricken to see the tears in Abola's eyes at Bijoy Chaliha's place even though Rupali's smile had taught me, "Do not trust, my friend – there is poison in your tears, no love… there is drama but no life."

I had heard the story of Rupali from Bijoy and if I express whatever he told in the form of a story, then it will be like this.

Rupali had come to Bijoy's house because of a cruel murder which occurred at Bilobari at night. Rupa's father was sentenced to imprisonment for thirty years and her mother was socially ostracized because of that horrific and bloody murder. I will narrate the incident based on what I got to know from Bijoy Chaliha.

There was a line of coolies near the hill about six miles away from the factory of Bilobari Tea Estate. These *Saotali* people were provided with a separate dwelling since they were very different from the *Mirjapuria, Kalahandia and Katakia* people in terms of their daily life, culture, norms, dialects etc.

The process of give and take had started and these people were very powerful. When they work hard under the scorching sun with their dark-complexioned, hairless and shiny bodies, their bosoms, hands and limbs seem like a portrait of some modern creative artist. They do not have too many clothes on except for a loincloth or a piece of cloth around the waist and on the head. They would wear a thick iron band on their hands. Their women were also structured in the same way – with strong and healthy stout figures to fight on an equal footing in every walk of life with the unlimited strength of the men. They did not try to beautify themselves with cosmetics nor did they learn any exercise or gaze that would awaken the animal instinct deep within people. But the stony soil turns into powder in the grip of their hands. Uncountable numbers of tea leaves enter the factory after having been plucked from the trees. There would be smoke from the chimney day and night and they would draw solace from the smell of raw tea leaves and dampened ripe tea leaves. They do not give importance to any particular part of the body. They would go to work with their uncovered, nude bodies and visit their neighbours in their 'line'. They would subvert the vulgar indications of some evil eye with a smile. The supervisors of garden conductors assign tough tasks to this class of people. I met one such man in the Bilobari Tea Estate who used to split wood at the office accountant's house six days per week and for six hours a day. He showed me the palm of his hands which could not be called palms as they were terribly cracked. He had bought a spoon to have his meals. Still, no one will find any slackness in their eyes and neither would there be any sharp realization. They would work for the garden by shedding their blood and, in return, they only needed money. Money was the only beloved object for them in their world.

Historical descriptions would consider them as non-Aryans. Overwhelmed with the great Jesus's words of love in the present and to enable them to meet God in heaven after their deliverance from hell in the future, some Brother of a common church initiated them into Christianity. I do not exactly know what changes occur after being baptized, but the names become completely different. The murderer father of Rupa, Marcus, used to stay in a colony near a hill under the Bilobari Tea Estate.

Even though he was an uneducated Saotal coolie, he was very well-natured and well-behaved. According to Assistant Manager Bijoy Chaliha, Marcus had certain good characteristics; for example, his stout healthy figure, a beautiful wife and the best-looking girl in that area. He was able to earn a fair amount of money indirectly on account of the first two and Marcus became a favourite for some of the Sahibs and excitable Babus on account of the third.

The Saotal women have tattoos on their hands, forehead and necks and they believed that it enhances their beauty. And the only woman who did not have tattoos on her body was fortunate Maria, Marcus' wife. I saw her only once during my weeklong stay at Bilobari Tea Estate. Though she had crossed three decades, she still could not be overlooked in the poetic expressions of some poets. No one could tell that she was the mother of a young adolescent like Rupa.

When I tried to see through my imagination, blending my observation with the description by Chaliha, I saw an unexpressed romantic story at the beginning of Marcus and Maria's married life. If someone were to read the expressions in her eyes, laced with beauty and abundant desire, then it will be like, "Food, food, food, my flame is not extinguished." Most probably, it was while fuelling the towering flame of her desire that Gauranga was burnt into ashes and the story of *Sinnamosta*[12] was born from these very ashes.

The introduction of Gauranga becomes necessary here.

About six years ago, Marcus had come to Assam, that is to the Bilobari Tea Estate, along with his wife as a gimitiya of three years. The tea gardens were like heaven for them, but their dreams were broken when they saw the muddied waters, unhealthy and unhygienic environs, the back-breaking hard labour and the harsh behaviour and exploitations of their employers. They composed poems while wiping their sweat and pouring cold water on their bellies:

Keeping us alive, is tea liqueur and roast rice

To Assam, they lied and sent us

Still, the affection they had towards their land would beckon them every day. Their fields called out to them and the sun did not see them rolling on the mud of their land. The land was mortgaged under Chaudhury Mahajan. They would pour out the blood of their own heart in the tea gardens here to die peacefully in their land; they would pour the milk of their thirst. Their girmit never ended – and even after working with their entire beings for a year, they did not have even two rupees in their hands.

Whatever it was, Marcus spent his days routinely with his daughter Rupa and wife Maria. Though they did not have the requisite situation, education or time to articulate the poems of love under the snowy moonlight of the winter, they wanted to go back to their land as soon as possible. He would be irritated with the behaviour of the scoundrel *Sahibs* here. There was some profit in working on one's own land. Rather than own work, they had become servants of others here who

---

[12] A form of goddess feared for her beheaded form

were also enjoying the profit. He could see the unfairness in such a system but there was no other option.

Three years after they arrived, Gauranga came to Bilobari Tea Estate on a new lease. He introduced himself saying that Marcus was his 'elder brother' from before.

Benign and innocent Marcus too heartily welcomed him as his brother. Gauranga was allotted a bachelor's house as he was unmarried. After Gauranga's arrival, the familiar sun soon started hiding many times on the other side of the bamboo grove coming out of the shirish and *jhao* tree afar. The evening wind distributed the din and the sounds of the drums of the coolie lines amongst the buds of the tea trees. Gradually, time made Gauranga old.

The British officers of the tea gardens built a central club for their leisure and would spend a day or two days in a week there for their own enjoyment. They were often seen playing tennis or polo on the lawns but no one knew what actually happened behind the curtains. The workers of the club would sit yawning or whiling in the cold breeze while they would dance, nude and crazed, to the rhythm of gramophone or piano while consuming costly liquor.

In certain places, some *Kala Sahibs*[13] also went with these *Boga Sahib*[14] officers to dance rhythmlessly. My friend Bijoy Chaliha had been inducted into this association. I got to know this from Abola. With the furry Alsatian and a racket in his hand, he said while starting his car: "I am off right to the club now, chum. Must have a jolly time with my Abola." Abola waved him bye with the tip of her sador.

A bird chirped in a mango tree far away. Though the gardeners and bearers stayed in the bungalow, they always

---

[13] 'Dark-skinned' officers
[14] 'Fair-skinned' officers

maintained a respectable distance from their owners. Therefore, the Sahibs and the Memsahibs did not feel their presence or existence. Maybe that was why Abola said: "Now we are alone, Tarun da".

I felt affectionate towards the afternoon. I found Abola after so many years today. There was a resurgence of old stories at the cusp of the end of an old chapter and the beginning of a new one. Memsahib Abola seemed like a small girl in my eyes. She stood behind my chair and, leaning her head, asked me: "Have our pasts died?"

The known lovely fragrance of her hair fell on my nostrils. I did not have anything to say to this naive girl. The unwritten and unexpressed stories had awakened her buried pains. She looked into my eyes while rubbing my chin. After that…?

After that Abola suddenly hugged me tightly around my neck and kissed me. I extricated her forcefully.

Abola!

She again wanted to hug me forcefully, "I want to make this evening of ours forever enduring, Tarun da. I am happy… I am happy Tarun da!

"Abola… Abola… *Chiii*"!

"How will you understand, Tarun da? You are a doctorate. You have seen green leaves and flowers, but you have not seen the bitter reality inside. He will come tonight without any self-control and will grab me like a demon. How will you understand those hellish torments, Tarun da?

"Abola, you are needlessly becoming anxious. You are doing something crazy." I did not want to harm the respect of the *Memsahib* of the Assistant Manager of this estate by pointing out her mistake at this vulnerable moment. But I felt pity for such a composed and pleasant soul like her, who had such a Vesuvius hidden inside her. Prosperity had not brought her peace. If she would ever get the chance of holding her own child in her lap, only then, perhaps, would peaceful waves flow over her aggrieved soul.

Abola's episode kept me away from the appeals of Rupali's tears for some time. This world overflows with the stories of many women, the tears of many adolescent girls and the laughter of many young girls. Abola- Maria- Rupali.

That portion of the story of Marcus in which the issue reached its ultimate point still remains. There was a huge chaos outside his bungalow on that dark night (it was a Sunday). Just sometime after that, the bearer entered the house screaming insanely, "Sir, Sir! Murder, murder…!"

The man was trembling like anything.

He went outside in his house attire.

"Who is there?"

Two sculptures were standing in the dark. The sky was about to sleep against the backdrop of still silence filled with the terror of death. There was a chorus of grasshoppers and insects in the flower garden.

"Who is there?"

The sculptures came forward. What transpired in the light made Assistant Manager Bijoy Chaliha's face contort in unknown terror.

A man, with a horrific and terrible appearance, put down a bag and an axe on the ground. There was the imprint of hellish pain in his face and eyes. His entire body was bloodied. Blood…Blood! Behind this ugly horrific murderer, was standing motionless, nude and humiliated, a woman with a deathly pallor. She tried to cover her body and face with her bloodied and torn saree but the part up to her knee was naked. She was trembling like anything.

The person was known to us. Benign and innocent Marcus. The woman was Maria – the healthy and beloved worker of Bilobari Tea Estate. Marcus opened the bag with a great deal of patience. Bijoy closed his eyes shut and sat down on the ground seeing the thing that toppled out of the bag. It was the head of a human being!

The head which was just beheaded from its body was Marcus' brother Gauranga's – it had been split in the middle with parashu's[15] axe. The blood of a common labourer spread like a red powder over the clothes and head, like an adhesive. The beheaded person alive just a few moments ago had become silent. It was perhaps the extreme conclusion of a hellishly bloody story.

When Bijoy regained his sense, he immediately called the Manager, "Cold-blooded murder! Please come right now to my bungalow. Here is the couple standing…Police…Yes… sending Head Clerk immediately to the police station."

After the call, Bijoy told them, "You all sit for some time."

Bijoy asked his watchman to keep an eye on them and went inside.

After that, everything was done as per the law. Before hearing the judgement of his thirty years of imprisonment, Marcus had said in his defence, "Gauranga was corrupt. My woman is also a slut - she is a *liar*."

An innocent Saotal labourer had rewarded unfaithfulness with murder. He did not recognize Maria as his wife. She was a prostitute.

Marcus had told his *Bor Sahib* and *Chot sahib* the story of his murder. Gauranga was his brother. Maria was his wife – married as per rituals. Behind the veneer of a relationship, both of them had lied to Marcus. Marcus kept busy with physical labour most of the time and only wished for some rest upon returning home from work, barely conscious after consuming

---

[15] Allusion of Parashuram perhaps

local liquor. Even though he kept scolding senselessly, he had the warmth of his mind. He liked to be noisy.

Marcus was a healthy, powerful, adult man. He knew that he had never kept Maria away from the pleasures of the body ever since the day of their marriage. But certainly, it was on account of some ill fortune that Maria's plump body and her full bosom burnt with a flame of desire. Or maybe her unsatiated desires, seeking a change in taste, were in search of an opportunity and therefore, she could smell the hilly soil of her land in the body of the newcomer Gauranga. She saw in his muscular shoulders and strong teeth, the image of a carnivorous animal. The fire burnt even more strongly and the hellish story of Maria and Gauranga went on for two years. Marcus never noticed this extremely secretive act.

But sin cannot be hidden away for long. The beginning of the last scene of this illicit act started that evening.

Marcus returned home after some entertainment, a little rest and visiting his neighbours on that Sunday. No one had the time to ask where Rupa was at that time. Surrounded by darkness, the small hut seemed to have the extreme silence of the cemetery. It seemed no one was there. He went inside and it seemed he was tormented by the pain of his breathing being obstructed. He saw in silhouette, indistinctly suspended between belief and disbelief, a scene which — if it had been perceived by Vonticelli or Descartes, would have been depicted as a horrendous picture of a poisonous, incensed python wrapped around the entire nude body of a woman against a dark background. As Marcus tried to breathe while standing over that doorstep which was sullied with the smell of sweat and lusty union, he saw Gauranga jump over him with a beastly demeanour. Experienced with the usual instincts of non-Aryans, Marcus also moved forward with his axe fast and flawlessly. Even before Maria managed to arrange her clothes and could scream, she saw a head immediately detached from its body overflowing with blood, which made the floor muddy.

Bijoy had said, "After that, I brought Rupa here." Maria has been ostracized from society now – people hate her. A new history may also be created for Rupa, a Saotal labour child. But the world is still pious in her eyes, laughter still pure, and she was not spoiled by the infamy of the illicit love relationship of her mother. She should still be pure with the fatherly love and simplicity of Marcus, accused of manslaughter. Maria, with that abundant and lively body, had changed the course of her life on account of her own desires. Bijoy said that she was an ordained prostitute now.

She was no longer aware of the life she had left behind. She no longer thought about Rupa also. Her home, body and mind now had all provisions to earn off her body.

The day I left the Assistant Manager of Bilobari Tea Estate Bijoy Chaliha's house, his land master arrived to take me to the station, "Wait, Tarun da" *Memsahib* ran towards me. Abola put an *indramalati* [16] in the buttonhole of my coat.

There were a few green leaves in the flower. Rupali was standing far away looking at us keenly.

✳ ✳ ✳

---

[16] A flower, like chrysanthemum

KUKUR

(DOG)

The labour contractor of Gopalpur Tea Garden, Dimbeswar Bora was taking rest in the armchair made of hessian cloth, after having had his lunch in the portico of his quarters. The one o'clock bell for the garden time has just rung in the factory. Within one hour, he will have to be present in the factory. Bora leaned into the armchair and, extremely relaxed, he closed his eyes and sucked at the tobacco pipe while attempting to blow away the tiredness of the forenoon with the smoke.

The first half had not gone well. Did it have to rain that much even if it was the monsoon? There was torrential rain. Moreover, thunder and lightning too. The male and female labourers did not have any portion of their bodies dry! What was the use of the umbrella-like japi on their heads? There was rainwater gushing through the ends of the tender leaves growing atop the lush tea shrubs. There was water seeping even in the knots tied around their waists.

The bell was rung early in the first half because of the heavy rains. The sun was peeping out since afternoon. The clothes of the labourers must have been half-dried by now. As soon as the bell rings, they will move hurriedly to their workplace.

The damp air had made the room chilly. The house, bereft of a fourth member, was engulfed in a screaming silence. Only the sound of Bora's smoke was heard- *turuk turuk* and that of Mrs. Bora having lunch in the kitchen.

Suddenly, there was a crackling sound at the door. Mr. Bora's eyelids naturally opened and he saw Boli entering the room drenched in water.

"Oh, God! Where had you been?"

Drops of water were flowing down his body. Bora could not bear it anymore and started wiping out the water in his eyes, forehead and body with the gamusa[17] he had on himself. Boli too made whining sounds as he decided to get his master's affection. "I called you many times… So many times! Why do you go here and there? See? How he is trembling?" Boli could find the warmth of his master's love in that disciplining. And, given that he had been born a dog, Boli responded to it by shaking his tail and licking Borah's feet.

Boli.

For common people, he may be a dog. A stray dog. But for Mr. Bora and Mrs. Bora who have been childless even after fourteen years of marriage, Boli was the third member of the family. He was not just an animal. Even though Boli was mute, he had not been deprived of the love due to a human child. In fact, he got more than his due. Mrs. Bora gave him all her love and affection much like a mother gives to her own child born out of her own womb. Boli had occupied a special place

---

[17] 'Gamusa' literally translates into 'something to wipe the body with', as 'ga' in Assamese means body and 'musa' is the infinitive form of 'wipe'. It is a rectangular piece of white cloth traditionally woven with red motifs on its shorter sides and borders on its longer sides. The gamusa is however used in multiple ways: it finds use as an object of reverence as the sacred book is usually placed on a gamusa and it is also used to cover the altar of a prayer house. Gamusa is worn by male Bihu dancers around the head and also used by farmers, fishermen etc. Elders are often offered gamusas during Bihu (specially Bohag Bihu which marks the spring festival) and traditional Assamese households still offer the gamusa to visitors as a mark of affection. The gamusa has received the Geographical Indication tag of Assam in 2022.

in their house. He has already spent five years in the house of labour contractor Dimbeswar Bora.

Nobody could remember who had left a spotted furry puppy in front of their gate some years ago.

Slowly, the puppy crossed the threshold and entered their house. He drank milk - ate bread, and ate rice. With time, it was seen that the puppy had not just entered their home – but without Mr. and Mrs. Borah's knowledge, he was able to occupy a place in their hearts too. Now, they worried about him as much as they would worry about a member of the family: rice had to be bought for him; fish or chicken had to be arranged for him; the blanket on his bed had to be hung out in the sunlight… there were so many things to be taken care of. It was as if, without Boli, there was nothing there in that house… When Borah returned from work he would call: "Boli!" When he left for work, "Boli!" When he sat for meals, "Boli!" It was only "Boli! Boli! Boli!" all the time.

Boli would climb onto their laps, jump up to the neck and follow Mrs. Bora while wagging his tail. No one could realise the importance of Boli's presence in the life of Mr. and Mrs. Bora who had not seen the face of their own child even after undergoing lots of religious rituals, treatments, incantations and engaging quacks.

Mr. Bora was a labour contractor and would remain busy with the work schedule of the garden in both halves of the day. The young boys and girls, engaged with work, would keep chattering away. Eight or nine-year-old kids would tie infants in a bundle and walk beside the mothers to quench their thirst at the breast. Fleeting winds would play hide-and-seek amidst the leaves of the *shirish*, the flowering *sonaru* and the shrubs. The budding tea leaves would simmer in the golden sunlight. The heart's forest would tremble and dreams would make an appearance in the buxom body of some nameless adolescent labour girl. In the minuscule world of two leaves and a bud, these were verdant images of love.

Bora would spend his days joking with and scolding these labourers amidst this busy environment of the garden. And at the same time, an anguished quietness would prevail in the small mud hut. That house was Bora's and Mrs. Bora would be alone then.

To get rid of the loneliness and that restless mind, she would keep herself busy with lots of work or she would read books. She would be engaged in her vegetable garden. Earlier, the children of the neighbours who worked as clerks or contractors used to get together and play with her. She would shower them with love, make dolls for them and would prepare *pitha* and other eatables for them. She heard a rumour about herself around that time – that Mrs. Bora was an ill-fortuned woman.

"She does not have children. Who knows? Some day she may tie up our children inside her house without our knowledge and give them poison."

Some mothers would scold their children by saying, "What potion has that old hag given you that you can't stay at home?"

After hearing such horrible remarks, she could gather neither the enthusiasm nor the courage to play with the children again. Earlier she used to visit her neighbours too and have small talk over a betel nut and leaf. Now there was a barrier even for that little merriment. Mrs. Bora was very lonely now.

After being in the noisy environment of the factory the whole day, Bora would come back home and feel as if that was not a home - rather it was the quiet cemetery of the night. No individual, who had not seen the face of his own child after fourteen years of marriage, would feel any attraction to coming back home.

An empty house, a void life and a tired body. They were just spending one day after the other with the pace of a pair of cattle thrashing paddy. Around just that time that furry rotund dog entered their lives to give love, to pour out the emotions of fatherhood and to give some solace to the motherhood that had been trapped breathless in the dark caverns of that barren womanhood. It was as if he was God's blessing. It was as if a steady, eternal and sprightly pace had fallen upon the trapped stream of life force.

It became possible to feel the presence of a third member in the family. It was as if some wildflower had spread a cool fragrance, even if the heart's blossom had not received the pride of being a sunflower. 'Boli' became the third prime member of the household.

There was no news of Boli till Bora finished his lunch today. Earlier they would have lunch together and his presence was therefore confirmed in the afternoons. But he had been creating some trouble at times this month. A group of dogs had come from somewhere and were making a din in the pathway. It was as if he was the leader of the pack. Where had he come back from now, all drenched?

Bora wiped his body, wrapped his hookah pipe up and took him towards the kitchen to feed him.

✻ ✻ ✻

Manager Sahib had written the letter.

"Mr. In-Charge Babu,

I will be happy to see you at my place today evening. Please convey my and Memsahib's regards to Mrs. Babu."

This incident had never happened in his life: the Manager himself had sent a personal letter to Dimbeshwar Bora! After reading the letter, Bora began to tremble out of excitement at this unexpected turn of events. He was sweating like anything. What was the matter? What was this incident?

There were murmurs here and there, and within two hours, everyone in the office got to know about it. Those who knew how to read English – especially the cursive handwriting of the Sahibs – came to Bora to read the letter and take pleasure in it. Others too touched it with their own hands. It was a personal letter. Surely, there was something to it!

"Ok, so did Bora guess something?"

What was there to guess? What personal matter could a Manager have with a labour contractor? When Mrs. Bora got to know about this, her face blackened like some herb that had been ground: "I feel he will be suspended from his job. It seems we have something inauspicious over our fates. Otherwise, would the Sahib send such a letter?"

It was made out as if it was not a letter but a notice terminating his job. Mrs. Bora, who was frequently anguished, felt her heart darken with the shadow of an unknown terror. Labour contractor Bora also got stressed. The head clerk had already declared that it was for the first time in Gopalpur Tea Estate that a Manager had sent a personal letter to his staff.

Unexpected!

Bora returned in the evening from Sahib's bungalow. From afar, he could see a few Babus from his office colleagues already present in the courtyard of his quarter. They had been waiting anxiously for his arrival to get the news. It was as if Bora would give them information about some train accident at some far-away place in which their relatives had also been involved.

"What happened, Bora? Tell us quickly." It seemed as if they would swallow him whole.

But Bora replied unenthusiastically, "Nothing, you know. It is nothing important. He just called me to talk."

Unbelievable!

They were waiting with bated breath and that too seemed to have stopped mid-way. Almost as if some magician had muttered something and kept a thousand rupees inside a box in front of an enraptured audience only to open it again and show that it was all gone!

Unbelievable!

This time Bora said willingly, "Means the Sahib said that the Memsahib had heard about our Boli from somewhere and felt love for him. Therefore, they wanted to keep him in the bungalow. They have asked for him tomorrow."

Pah! They thought it had something to do with the kingdom and he was telling them that the bats had finished the bananas! They left the place tired and it seemed that blood circulation had returned to Mrs. Bora's pale face which now turned lively. God has saved them for this time.

A smile appeared on Mrs. Bora's face when Bora revealed a secret: Sahib had patted his back and said that from the next month, his salary will be increased by Rs. 5!

✳ ✳ ✳

There is a sweet admixture of happiness, sadness, as well as pride in preparing one's own children for war by feeding and dressing them with their own hands. But there could only be agony, the pain of separation and grief for a childless couple who had to give up a mute living being who had occupied a larger portion of their hearts. It was only natural for a dog to leave a home. But…

It is a matter of realization, a very simple experience of life. For lakhs of years, we carried you in our heart and yet the heart was not enough.

Bora bathed Boli with his own hands in the afternoon and brushed him. Mrs. Bora fed him rice with milk. Bora joked: "Boli will become a foreigner from today. He will have biscuits and meat and will roam around in cars. He will stay in Sahib's bungalow. Good! It is for the better. What do you say?"

"Indeed. He must have been a good soul. The daughter of a woodcutter will go to a king's son. Eat child, for the last time you are eating in this broken house."

He was a dog - how would a dog feel the extreme pain of a barren couple? He did not know where he would be after four hours.

In the evening, Bora himself took Boli to the Manager's bungalow. Both Sahib and the Memsahib were waiting outside their bungalow. They passed a smile at Bora to show their happiness. A bearer took Boli inside.

Bora gave a humble namaskar and returned. He had with him on the way back a heavy mind and an empty heart. Boli was no longer there. But…

Suddenly, the sound of a gunshot shattered his heart and broke it into two.

There was an immediate helpless sorrowful cry that followed. –ke—e—e—e—u. What had happened? Bora felt it beyond his imagination. He began to tremble and he felt dizzy.

Whose cry was that? Whose cry?

Unconsciously, he looked back towards the bungalow. It seemed the sound of the gunshot had come from that direction. That would mean the Sahib had shot and killed Boli! But why? why? For what fault of his had the Sahib shot Boli? Bora clutched his head and sat down on the floor. His unspoken pain fell in the form of tears which gushed down his face.

Traitor…!

"Boli has been killed. Boli has been shot dead by the Sahib. Boli is no more. Oh…oh." Bora walked towards his home unsteadily.

In the meanwhile, somebody had already informed Mrs. Bora about something. It seems Boli had bitten Sahib's foreign dog in the afternoon yesterday and had torn it to pieces. The Sahib had himself taken it to the hospital. The Sahib was burning with rage on getting to know that his foreign dog had been bitten.

Mrs. Bora was eagerly waiting for Bora at the threshold of their home standing there alone. He had not returned yet. Yesterday he informed her that his salary had been increased by five rupees. What could he possibly say today?

Mrs. Bora's petite brain was still unable to comprehend that their beloved Boli had to accept a death sentence for biting a foreign dog.

✳ ✳ ✳

(THE TRAUMA OF THE CAPTIVE)

In the desert world of sands, the hot summer breeze creates mirages and, with the gateway of dreams, the countless astonishing stories of many a wordless maiden welcome one. My dusty tale of this Rupali… the rhythm of its poetry that seeks to disappear… the cadences of the song that end shivering… I want the world to be illuminated with these… it should be illuminated more.

A lamp is alit in a small hut in the coolie line beside the hill. A well-structured face shimmering in the half-light and shadow.

Before that – oh there was a girl. She was not a princess – not a princess of the forest – a very simple girl. Let us assume her name was Rupa –Rupa(li). The glow of the sun will hide through the bamboo grove like the smile of a proud naughty girl that comes out after many efforts. The day had made the Bilbari Tea Estate cry a lot without being asked. Shirish, *medelua* and the brimming tears of 'two leaves and a bud' made the pathways overflow. It was the time of full leaves now. The smell of life, the smell of living life, is there in the fragrance of the raw leaves. She sat down under the public tube well in her wet body right after having weighed the leaves at the leaf factory. She will wash her body. Taking a bath nearby was Rajana – her friend. Rajana pushed her as a prank.

Damn! Rupa drew a cross near her chest and, laughingly, ran away from there in her wet clothes. Reaching home, she searched for the small kerosene lamp and lit the lamp wick with the matchstick. In the partial light and shadow, a well-formed face lit up. Rupali's face. Rupa knew that her husband won't come in the evening. There was some meeting in the middle of the line.

The meeting was held on account of a tree. The name of their locality was '1 Number Pahar[18] Line'. It was beside the hill. Earlier it seems wild boars, elephants and wolves used to come and disturb them at night. They only said, "Basti, we won't leave." We will not leave the village. They wouldn't leave this village primarily because of 1 Number Line only. Many years ago, Rupa's grandfather and great-grandfather had started their girmitya life in this deserted region. Many days passed after that. Many babies were born there. Many young boys and girls! They work, celebrate festivals, play Holi, bury when someone dies, and kick up a dance frenzy after consuming laopani[19] at marriages. The wheel of the chariot moves on.

This is 1 Number Pahar Line of Bilobari Tea Estate. A group of people held some rituals by clearing out the base of the peepal tree in their locality many days ago. They would gather around the base of that tree; get involved in fights there; the girls dance there to the rhythm of drums holding each other by the neck. The night watchman would give the work schedule for the next day under that tree. When some Sahib or Babu comes, they would stand there under its shadow since no other place was as clean as that. If the crazy wind of Phagun destroys someone's house, then they seek shelter under that very tree.

It was the peak season of raw tea leaves in the garden. The factory was running day and night. There was a din. The *Bor*

---

[18] Hill

[19] Traditional rice beer.

Sahib[20] called the Head Overseer and said, "A letter has come: the import of coals will be decreased by 60% from next month. The solution? We cannot keep the factories closed. The market is in demand. The ships are calling at the port to take the cargo of tea leaves, the train engines are kept running at the stations. The solution? All the available trees in the garden should be cut down to arrange the firewood."

Groups of labourers knocked down giant trees with knives and axes. Some of them felt as if the burning of history had begun. The young boys who usually frequented the garden in search of jobs noticed that the Bilobari Tea Estate has begun to seem empty now; it seemed forlorn.

One day, a tractor came and hit a peepal tree. The peepal tree, the kin of the 1 Number Pahar Line, which was the only source of happiness and sorrow, laughter and tears for many generations began to tremble before it had begun to spread its shadow. The glue from the trunk of the tree began to flow down like the blood of a great warrior being wounded by weapons. A huge strike. 'G–o–n––e'.

The labourers shouted gleefully. Everyone who had been watching bowed – they paid tribute to the tree who was like their parent, for the last time. Then everybody's eyes brimmed with tears. They must have cried.

That Phukan Babu—the new labour Babu. He had occupied the hearts of the workers, and labourers of Bilobari Tea Estate within just one month. Phukan Babu had two surprising properties—firstly his face and secondly his eyes.

He had untiring working calibre and a sense of obduracy in his eyes. Rupali could still remember that day. It was the heavy rains of autumn. They objected, "It is very difficult to pluck leaves in such rains. It should be closed." Supervisor

---

[20] Senior Officer

Sahib did not listen to them, "That won't happen. Scoot, you scoundrels."

The group of ladies began to grumble. Rupali was one amongst them; everyone knew that she was fearless. Everyone digested her abuses since she was a beautiful female. "All the Sahibs will enjoy and we can't? We won't work. "She was about to throw her basket and come out but suddenly her gaze stopped. Phukan Babu.

He was looking at them with a thoughtful expression, under a tree in the heavy rains. The water was going through his clothes. He would squeeze out his wet handkerchief and rub his face time and again. The contours of his face and forehead were emotionless and nonchalant. Rupa was fascinated. Her anger turned to ice in an instant. "Babu, why didn't you bring an umbrella?"

Phukan didn't say anything. He smiled slightly. Money was required to buy an umbrella. He only got eighty rupees of silver coins. So… he again wiped his face, squeezing the hanky. His lips had become a bit pale. Though he objected, Rupa forcefully gave him her torn umbrella. She then made a turban out of the *sador* she used for plucking leaves over her head. Her bosom became visible with her bare blouse.

That was Phukan Babu.

It seems he had gone to the line at night many times and had told the main people there: "Why don't you all complain to Sahib?" He said that nowadays if the coolies, and labourers came together to complain, then even the Sahibs or the higher officers fear them.

The tree was cut down on Sahib's order. Now a kirtan ghar[21] should be built in that place. They will enjoy the rituals, and festivals and will hold meetings there. The children will

---

[21] Place of worship holding the holy book

play there. That Naam Ghor[22] will be the central point of their life circle. Phukan told them, "You all go and complain to Sahib."

The alarm rang at eight o'clock. The tea garden does not run according to the Indian Standard Time: it runs on the local time or garden time. The historical clock of Bilobari Tea Estate runs according to Bilobari time. After having worked for twenty-three years, the old head clerk's gait and that of the clock had almost the same rhythm. If some newly appointed young man asked, "Clerk Babu, the clock is moving too fast," displeased, he would say: "Who told you that? My clock syncs with the radio." The clerk replied gravely, "Leave it, this Bilobari garden does not run on your radio."

Rupa's husband has gone to the meeting and, after creating a clamour, he would lie down on the bed after having dinner. She filled the water vessel and put it on the stove: it was time for cooking. The fire burnt more when she put more firewood in it.

There was a knock at the door.

She was unaware. Her saliva flowed down her cheek and landed on the stool. Phukan Babu said, "Hey Rupa, you don't have to work in the garden. You work in my house. I am unable to manage alone." She giggled and walked away: "No *Babu,* my husband will beat me. He is a very angry man." He was an angry man and would beat her.

A man entered. He saw by the light of the lamp, that she was sleeping, having placed the end of her *saree* on the floor. The saliva from her lips had flowed over her cheeks. He waited for some time. He took out the hanky from his pocket and wiped her cheek. She did not move. Slowly, he lifted her underarm and tickled her hard.

---

[22] Place of worship in Vaishnavite tradition

He laughed out loud. Rupali's husband: "Hey, have you fallen asleep?"

Eh! She had fallen asleep. Damn! What a dream she had had! She felt a tingling sensation in her body. Then she arranged her clothes and started striking his back. "This man does not have shame. Chii… does not feel shame." She suddenly looked at the stove; the flame had gone out. The lentils in the pan had burnt away.

"Rascal! So much water. It was raining like anything." He washed his feet at the threshold.

During those rainy days, Phukan tied the hands and hearts of the people of *Pahar* line with some unknown chants. He gave them the source of nectar and he also gave them a way of living and dying together.

For the last thirty-three years, if there was one person whose signature could be seen in the official cash memos of Bilobari Tea Estate, then it was that of the Head Clerk's. "Only the clock knows the count of how many *Bor Sahib, and Chotsahib* I sent, how many were given employment and how many were sent back by this very hand. Nowadays, Matric Pass candidates come and act smart for a few days in front of me. But… He! He! He!" The young overseers could see the belly of the Head Clerk before him.

Two of his sons-in-law and two of his sons work in this very garden. Relatives were also there. The ears of the head clerk were alert, his eyes were sharp, and his tongue spoke in limits and the uncultured smile that came out through his moustache was the ultimate medicine.

Bokuli (the Head Clerk's father called her *bhekuli*[23] affectionately while young eligible bachelors called her Bokul) was the youngest daughter of the Head Clerk and his wife.

---

[23] Frog

There were two things to know about Bokuli. The first one was age and the second one was education. Since no one had any horoscope, when her mother said, "She must be around sixteen years or so," then everybody had to believe her. Whenever anyone asked about her education, then the answer was she had passed many Assamese, English classes. Her father wanted this pest of a child to get married to an eligible man, so he could get relief from this stress.

A jeep was seen coming through the path of the garden made yellowish with bricks. Some pedestrians took a peek. Their bodies shivered in some unknown terror. The car stopped directly in front of the Manager's office.

After some time, Phukan Babu entered the Manager's room. A police officer in light blue glass goggles and the Manager were sitting in the room. The third person was standing all cramped up. The police officer moved his chair slightly and asked, "Are you not Mr. Phukon?"

Phukon made a sound with his throat. The officer asked the second question, "Do you know this man?"

"He is the watchman of Bor line of our garden, Ramroton"

"That's good of you. Now listen to his statement."

The summary of the statement that Ramroton gave, trembling with folded hands is: He did not know the reasons for the chaos created by all the coolies in front of Bor sahib's bungalow for their not working, since the past three days that they were on strike. But he has seen Phukon Babu going to the line many times and talking to the people when he had gone there, to tell them about their work schedule.

The police officer asked him a third question, "For how many days have you been working here?"

"Most probably seven months."

"That is quite a bit, that is quite a bit". Then he looked at the Manager and asked, "Now Head Clerk please."

The Manager pressed the ebonite button with his index finger. After some time, the old Head Clerk came in, tucking the end of his dhoti into the pocket of the *Punjabi Kurta* and greeted both of them. The officer asked him respectfully, "Head Clerk *babu*, for how many years you have been working here?"

"Total thirty years, you know. He! He! … Total thirty years. This Sir is my fifth manager—He…He…He."

"Alright. Can you tell me how much trouble have these coolies of Bilobari Tea Estate created?"

He looked at Phukon obliquely and said, "Genuinely, they have never done even once. They are really stupid people, you know. They don't get any clue regarding all this."

Then the officer asked Phukon the fourth question, "Mr. Phukon, do you have anything to say?"

He thought for two minutes and said, "Me…no. I won't say anything."

Everybody fell silent suddenly.

"Ok. You can leave." Ramroton also went out as soon as he got an eye gesture.

Many office employees surrounded the Head Clerk and Phukon outside. Phukon was silent and pensive. A sense of severe hatred reflected in his face and eyes. The Head Clerk said with his familiar smile, "Something has been going wrong with the nation and time, you know."

The central point of the circle of the dispute was Bokuli – the youngest daughter of the Head Clerk. The Head Clerk had had a spurt of affection towards Phukan some two days after his joining in the garden. He often asked him to visit his place and advised him to consider his home as his own home to ask for a meal or tea. Phukan visited a few times for the sake of civility. It was then that he noticed Bokuli used to hover around whenever she saw Phukon and would act coy whenever she came to offer him tea, after having applied powder.

Phukon became alert. He got the rotten smell of a conniving mind.

Head Clerk noticed that the prey was going out of his hand: he was quite clever. Still, he could not trap Phukon despite all his tactics. One day, Phukon denied his invitation and informed him he would be happy if he would not get any more invitations in the future.

The people of the Pahar line went to the Manager and complained to him that day. They requested a Kirtan Ghar in that place with the help of government funds. The British officer became furious. "Leave, you scoundrels! This is our Tea Garden. This is my Tea Garden."

After the East India Company stepped into the heart of India, they created a section of people with the mindset and opinions like for example, that white-skinned people had rights over the whole world; that they were part and incarnations of God; black-skinned people had to be ruled by white-skinned people. Such beliefs were set in the coolies of the *Pahar line* The sun was at its peak then. The sound of the herd of cattle going to graze afar and the tinkling sound of the bell around their necks could be heard.

The number of male and female workers in the *Pahar Line* was three hundred and fifty. Phukon told these people, "You inform the people of the other lines. Let's see what *Sahib* does after all the people of these gardens come together."

This conversation as well as all the conversations with the people of the other lines had been heard by the watchman Ramroton. After that, it was heard by the Head Clerk who had been working for thirty-three years and then by his fifth Manager who was British. "The *Sahabs* are part and incarnations of your gods. They are omniscient. Otherwise, they would not have reached here crossing the seven seas and thirteen rivers to rule here. It is very difficult to fool them. What say? He…He…He!"

The matter of the police car coming to the garden and questioning Phukon Babu spread like wildfire. There was satisfaction in the Head Clerk's family. "So much pride in such a young boy. He was all swollen with pride at having landed a job in the garden. There you go now – have fun!"

Phukon had been given a notice to immediately leave the garden within sixteen hours. The forwarding had the signature of the Head Clerk.

The coolies of the garden who heard this news were all anguished. That evening, the young woman called Rupali broke into tears while lighting the evening lamp after having her bath. She, her man and three labourers of the line reached the small house in Phukon within one hour.

The train of thought may have been snapped for Phukon. He suddenly hurriedly on seeing them, and tried to smile.

"Raghu, Gopal you have come! O God! Why are you sitting on the floor? Sit on that bench there. Oh, Rupa! You have also come?"

"No Babu, it is fine. It is fine. I am getting a love of the soil by sitting on the floor near you. Happiness can be found in the dust and dirt too if there is love." Rupali went to the foot of his bed and stood there. She was covering her eyes.

Everybody was silent. A sound was coming from the factory. Noise and the sound of the drum could be heard far away as well as the din of the grasshoppers. Gopal asked, "You will go, *Babu?*"

He laughed. A sense of depression and hatred seem to have spread. "Won't a new Babu come after I leave?"

"Why do we need a new *Babu?* There were lots of new *Babus* here who became old now. But there was no one to think about our happiness and sorrow; to ask us to come out of the darkness and mud. The Babus are the chimneys of the factory, the Sahibs are the factory and we are the tea leaves. The juice of these tea leaves is our blood."

"All of you should always stay together always. One should speak up if the other is in trouble. Don't forget anyone as if they were some pebbles on a road. Don't ignore anyone."

"You have given us mantra; you have given us faith. But we are blind and you will not be our sarothi[24]."

Rupa whimpered. She was a common labour woman. She saw a star in her subconscious sky without her knowledge – now clouds had come and covered it. "We will never get a Babu like you. We will not get a person like you. I forgot about my happiness seeing you the other day and returned to my work all soaked in the rain. It is because you know how to cry for other people. How many people are there in this garden who can take the burden of others' misery on their shoulders? Not just me, every young man and woman started respecting you, started loving you. You will go tomorrow."

"Again, Ramroton will hear all this." They will get furious.

"We will cut Ramroton into pieces, Babu. That scoundrel. That traitor."

"When will you leave, Babu?"

"I have to leave the garden before 9 am tomorrow. The police have eyes on me."

They became silent again in the anguished moment of bidding goodbye. "These are common things." Phukon said, "You may not know. The world is changing now. There is a newness in people's thinking and perspectives. People are learning to stand against injustice. You will have to prepare yourself. There are lots of tea gardens in Assam. There are lots

---

[24] Charioteer: allusion to Lord Krishna.

of labourers in India. All of them – all of you – will have to learn to live as human beings. You will have to be enlightened with new days. You will have to be together for that."

They didn't say anything. They just kept staring at him.

"You go now, got it? Anyway, we will meet tomorrow morning. Please tell everybody in the line about me. I will not go today; I am not feeling good."

He did not say anything more. They got up despite their unwillingness to do so. Rupali looked at him. Her eyes seemed swollen. Her body was wrapped in a white *saree*. She may have not combed her hair after taking bath. She was ready to leave. But before that, she suddenly hugged Phukon's feet and touched her forehead to them. "I will never give my umbrella to any other Babu." Why had I given you my umbrella that day? For you, that was so much. But I am someone's married woman. But how can I deny the truth? How had there been so much space for you in my ignorant heart? I cannot explain.

Phukon pulled his feet away. "*Chi* Rupa, what will your man say? I am not a great man. Why are you seeking blessings from me?" He patted her head and kept his left hand folded for some time. After that, he unfolded it. "You go. Gopal is waiting for you."

"I will come again in the morning. I will come again in the morning. I will see you for the last time. Everyone from Bilobari Tea Estate will be there… the one who will not be there is you. Whom we want."

She went away. They too…

He lay down on the bed once again. He would sleep for one last time in this small house of Bilobari Tea Estate. The police would take responsibility by 9 am tomorrow. He had worked against the government.

He wanted to laugh.

The nightlife of the coolies was on. Meal, intoxication, *jhumur*... A mixed rhythm in the vulgarity and dust and dirt of life. Time was walking across the historical clock of Bilobari. It would dawn tomorrow. Above it...an azure sky will be brightened in sunshine... for one day... no, for many days... for all days... the sky will be brightened.

And, he will leave this garden forever...

✳ ✳ ✳

PHOOLMONI

(PHOOLMONI)

Phoolmoni

Phoolmoni of Sonajan. Sonajan.

Sonajan Tea Garden is filled with gold. The crazy dance of the monsoon was jumping through the innumerable tender leaves of *sirish* of the Sonajan garden. What an indescribable moment; it had only the cacophony of living life. To the unending rhythm of the clouds, was life's restless dance and din.

Lots of people searched for gold at Sonajan. (Men, women, young and old women, young boys and girls pluck – all would pluck two leaves and a bud). There would be conversations between work; the laughter and quarrels of the young ones; the superficial harsh order of the Sardar. The overseer would supervise. Between work, a mother would feed her baby, whom she had made sleep in the nearby alley. She would pluck leaves with one hand and placate the crying baby with another. Life lives on amidst a few hard and fast regulations. And lives on love and the eternal truths of the primitive world.

The pain of their birth is reflected clearly through their eyes and face.

A dream of this very Sonajan… It was a common matter and it was just at that moment that the womb for Phoolmoni's birth narrative had been created.

It should have been seen earlier, but I did not see it. I was standing and watching a long queue of about three hundred women proceeding slowly near the weighing place of tea leaves in the factory. One by one, they lifted their basket of tea leaves on the spring balance and then spread out the leaves in the spring room for withering.

Suddenly I noticed, holding on to a heavy basket with both hands and with the zeal of a hilly stream of the Bhado month, there was a seemingly crazed youth. The knee-length attire was still showing clearly the fleshy hips… a small effort to cover the greenery of the peak of a lofty hill.

Surprising…!

This was a brightened lighting in the dark black sky of Sonajan. It was an exception to see a healthy figure and a charming face amidst the common women of the tea garden. Visible through the light attire was seen a trembling, insatiable hunger.

I do not know why I went ahead and looked up her name in the register.

Phoolmoni.

A beautiful name. Phoolmoni is a flower: a complete blooming yellow flower of a green tea tree. No – it was the brightened bunch flowering in the *shirish* or the flowers of *gulmohar*. I was transfixed and stared for a few moments when she crossed.

The other women too passed by one by one. They will take rest for some time after having completed weighing of leaves. They had their food if, that is, they could arrange for it. Then would again have to go into the tea garden for the afternoon work.

I came back to my quarter and brought back with me the curiosity one has for a half-read book; a few like slithering snakes; a fire in the forest.

These snakes… So nasty… So appealing.

I did not see Phoolmoni for the rest of that day. Her plump body and her folded lips keep coming to my mind amidst my busy schedule too. There was no point in telling a lie; the picture of that crazy youth troubled my inexperienced mind till very late in the night.

Even in the midst of this contorted and melted desire, an exceptional feeling of Sonajan, filled with various trees, kept coming into my mind. A whimpering of the pain of having and not having something was there in the midst of the silence. I woke up listening to the harsh howls of the foxes and the horned owls; I went out and saw a strange forest of silence outside.

What tough propitiation of the night!

The Sonajan tea estate was sleeping with the unknown warmth of love by embracing the light of some twinkling stars in the sky far away.

I had perhaps seen a brutal combination of class distinction here. Sonajan was the smallest of worlds. I have seen life here and I had seen various types of anguish here. I had talked to the labourers and discussed many a crisis. Gradually, I came to speculate that these people also have a burning fire in their hearts. But they had no outside wind and it never burns in a big way. However, they go on living. But they never thought about how was it that they could live a good life. They had not had an opportunity to think about it. Maybe they could not get any opportunity.

I have seen the death of pigs, the death of hens, and the death of human beings in the labourer's line. I have heard from many people that except for diseases that require prescribing quinine and laxatives, doctors faced a dilemma for all other diseases. That doctor might consider a labourer as a hen as they did their job just to earn money and not to provide service to human beings through medical science.

The labourers would say that they thought they would get happiness in the garden. But they were misled. They did not know when their dreams will yield results. Till that happened, they would probably have to stay this way. That was why they would cry their heart out when someone dies and seek permission from the Sahibs to do the rituals for the expired ones. God had killed them, and it was not in their hands.

Do any of them wish that everyone should die? Yet, "God will kill everyone – everyone is sinful, *Babu*": this was Durgaboti's statement. The inextinguishable fire that Durgaboti has for Phoolmoni, a painful history which had been burnt into ashes could also be found in that.

* * *

This was the truth of old Durgaboti… the sordid story of the life that she had already left. Sonajan did not exist at that time. Durgaboti was a resident of Kirtigarh. The king Dhoromraj Rai Partab Narayon Bahadur was the king zamindar. He had lots of land and ryots[25]. Moreover, he had huge mansions, houses, horse chariots, vehicles and many queens. He was the owner of many temples and many children.

Durgabai went on saying: King Bahadur used to go to Poona sometimes and at other times to Delhi or Mumbai. Many big personalities used to come to Kirtigarh. Once, when a British officer came there for some governmental work, he had stopped at the flower garden of King Bahadur for an hour. Later, Partab Narayon constructed a beautiful statue at that place as a memorial.

---

[25] The term 'ryot' (also spelt as 'raiyat', 'rait' or 'ravat') was a general term throughout India to indicate a peasant, farmer or cultivator. 'Zamindars' were landlords who could typically hire ryots as hired labour. The system was different in various provinces of India. The ryotwari system went back to Mughal system of land control and was appropriated by the British who came up with the two systems of land control: Ryotwari and Mahalwari.

Lots of money was spent in the name of the flower garden of King Bahadur. The garden was known to all people. When big people hear about Kirtigarh state, they understood it to be a pleasing garden built by spending lots of money and labour: it was the flower garden of the palace.

Durgaboti went on to say. The companion of this flower garden was King Partab Narayon's youngest queen (*Chotrani*). There are age variations amongst the queens as they were earned at different periods. Some pleasure houses were constructed in the flower garden for the King's amusements. The King's Dewan[26] searched for beautiful women in the festivals and brought them as gifts for the King. (They were called *Chotrani* once they were brought to the palace). They were given pleasure houses to stay in. Then the King would come to the flower gardens in the evening and take a good look at the young women. The Dewan would spend this time in anxiety. When the King smiled in satisfaction, looking at the commodity, the Dewan too would smile. The Dewan's fortunes too, perhaps, would smile.

The waves of *tabla* and the twinkling sound of anklets would come from the pleasure houses of the King from that night till many days. The King would be involved in acts of love till dirty deadly weariness did not set in. Some hellish nights would pass by. For some mysterious reason, some poisonous insect would start to bite the King's brain and the solemnity of caves would descend on the pleasure house. The King would start feeling unhappy again until regular life would start all over again.

And *Chotrani.*

Gradually, the situation came to such a pass that the *Chotrani* would not take care of the hundreds of flowers around

---

[26] Minister

her and the King did not need her anymore to take care of all his needs. Instead of all this, there would be endless leisure and the contriving of a conniving mind; the beginning of a new life in which they would entertain government servants by serving them betel leaves and dangling their long earrings at them. A new flower would join the earlier brigade.

The yelping of the young labourers, along with the bellows of drunkards and the howling of the foxes in the tea garden, time would trudge along the bell hung at the verandah of the factory. A night would end. Old Durgaboti, who comes out to guard the children's home beside the hospital, stood near the crossroad. Sonajan would start dancing in the eyes of Durgaboti who would look to the sky where some birds were flying.

—Sonajan. Assam Desh[27].

—Kirtigarh.

Hundreds of tides of the dark stories of the life left behind start to make Durgaboti's eyes clouded. Sonajan had never come even to her dreams some nine years ago.

But a mistake has been committed.

No, it is not a mistake of Durgaboti. This is not even a mistake of Phoolrani aka Phoolmoni. Then whose mistake was it?

As a result of which mistake were the erstwhile citizens of King Rai Partab Narayan Bahadur of Kirtigarh now searching for the lost past in the soils of Assam? This was the mistake of the star in some other sky tainted by some fallen meteors. Now that stain is still there in the sticky soil of Sonajan. The forest fire of the life left behind remained, as irritable traces whose simmers had not yet died out.

---

[27] Nation/region

The birds were still playing in the sky. Durgaboti threw down the flying bird of her mind in the sky of Kirtigarh on the grass of Sonajan. She walked towards the crèche house.

✳ ✳ ✳

I saw Phoolmoni again. I don't know why I felt a thrill from seeing her.

"Phoolmoni, you are my dream. You are the wild breeze of the crazed Phagun of my heart."

She passed by me with swift steps. The green body of her youthfulness was trembling along with her steps. Phoolmoni was a cup of old grape juice. Phoolmoni was the sweet smell of a sweaty blouse. Phoolmoni was not a door of the church. Who knows, maybe she had been, she must have been born for that.

Yes…it seems that is why an accident occurred.

The challenge of Narayon for his father Partap Narayon by establishing all the games of dice of his manhood can be considered an accident. That was the mistake. That is the stigma. It is one ofthe dirtiest incidents of Kirtigarh palace which has been there, generation after generation. There is only a single difference.

That is the terrible mystery of Kirtigarh. It may be a rumour.

To this day, some footsteps are heard in an isolated room away from the palace. The cries of the trapped life of a spirit come out, breaking the silence of the night…a mysterious lock up of Kirtigarh.

Nobody has ever thought about it for a single day… the cut of an axe on the dignity of the lock-up and pleasure house of Kirtigarh. Ugly and melted… stinking.

It was good luck.

Two things come to rescue Phoolmoni from the dirty boundaries of the palace of Partab Narayon: 'a train' and 'an agent of a Tea company in Assam.'

It was only because she had taken that good fortune in her fist that till this day, Phulmooni took a resolution as a woman in the verdant tea garden of Sonajan – of living with peace and satisfaction. But people always commit one mistake: to think that the crazy ones live in one corner of the world.

* * *

I received a letter from the head office of the company through the manager after two years of my service.

"…in view of your involvement in some anti-social work in the garden… in view of your attacking the dignity of the tea company and standing against the manager and being engaged in activities detrimental to our interest and your suspicious behaviour (called movement in English) in a few places, why would the authority not take action against you? Therefore, the company expressly wishes for you to leave the garden within 48 hours of receiving this notice."

I do not feel the necessity to prepare the elaborated list on what basis the company had sent me this notice. Still, this important news will come out in the important story of Phoolrani aka Phoolmoni.

One evening, Dugaboti Burhi and her daughter Phoolmoni visited my house as a result of the trust they had in me. I had called them. Because, if I had to write the birth story of Phoolmoni, I needed to know the conclusion too. But they had no notion that I was planning a conspiracy to publish a story on them. But they were happy with just one thing: that there was at least one person who was willing to know their painful story.

If a tiny flash of light coming through a small window of a closed room brightens their life filled with the smoke of the factory of Sonajan and the dust of the path, then, there was no harm in it. Let it brighten!

By pressing the soft calf of her right leg, Phoolmoni went on saying how on a quiet afternoon she was taken up forcefully in the 'fashion palki'[28] of King Partab Narayon. When the bearded wrestler with a huge turban began to tear the end of her *Saree* and pressed it forcefully into her mouth, she became senseless.

Durgaboti *Burhi* went out of my room wiping her tears at that moment. I did not know what games of shadows had started in the thin light of the lamp. I became motionless.

…When she got her sense back, she found herself lying on a soft bed in a dark room. She could not realize how far the sun has already moved. She came to know about her disastrous condition when she tried to arrange her clothes. Suddenly, she got up and sat on the bed.

"…You scoundrel, shameful…"

The curtain of darkness was still there before her eyes.

A young woman, Phoolrani. She had grace in her body; dreams in her mind, green dreams. And she had lots of time to gift as a return of love.

But everything became befuddling.

And because of this befuddling, she did not know where she was. What was the time now? Because of this befuddling, she did not get to know what the snake in front of her was bringing towards her.

That is when a huge mistake happened.

It was nothing new in the decaying history of Kirtigarh: the rape of a beautiful passing girl and destroying the dignity

---

[28] Palaquin

of her womanhood and virginity in the lock-up. And the story of that captured prey, Phoolrani, wasmerely the repetition of the old one.

Durgaboti Burhi had not returned yet.

—suddenly the door opens; a shadow came forward in heavy and unsteady steps. Phoolrani saw a shadow of someone, a spirit. It may be a venomous snake-like death with all the poisons of this dirty world. She kept staring at it in disbelief.

Suddenly there was a flash of light. The man threw a bright light in her face. A vulgar body of a woman was still sitting steadily because of the darkness.

"Ha…ha..ha…My sweet…"

Snake…Snake…Snake. Phoolrani tried hard to cover her body. The shadow came forward. She wanted to hide in bed itself. But…

"Don't be scared; my love."

What a nasty… devil.

"I am the prince. Prince Samudra Narayon."

Prince Samudra Narayon? The first child from the first wife of King Dharamraj Rai Partab Narayan Bahadur. He was very notorious. Samudra Narayon grabbed her in her left hand. —a terrible scream.

Some burning moments. In the light of the torch, was seen like some figure of hell with a whip in one hand, Maharaj Partab Narayan! Even before she could realize what had happened, Partab Narayan hit Rajkumar Samudra Narayon in the stomach which sent him reeling. The King entered – Phoolrani tried to curl up and hide in one place. Such audacity to intervene in the property of the king? At such a moment, Rajkumar got up and attacked the king hitting his neck with a huge blow.

This! This was a golden opportunity! While they were fighting over a piece of meat, the prey escaped through the open door. Even before the sentry got wind of it, Phoolmoni had run far away. Her village was three hours away. It was familiar. The night was dark.

The events after this were short.

When Phoolmoni reached home in the middle of the night, her mother was unconscious. The daughter that had gone missing had been caught by the King's hooligans and the fact that this was nothing strange in the Kirtigarh private state had been made known to her mother by a few people in the village, which had agitated Durgaboti. Phoolrani said that it was only after her mother had examined each part of her body like a doctor that she had been assured of her virginity.

At the crack of dawn the next day, they left the village in fear and took shelter in the house of a relative about twenty likes away. There they met the agent of the tea company of Assam Desh. They got to know about the opportunities to live in Assam with wealth and happiness from him. The Sahibs themselves will talk to them…etc…etc.

That was Durgaboti. That was Phoolrani.

Yes. Phoolrani's name was registered in the government record as Phoolmoni.

Both of them went back that night.

It is true that I had quite a weakness for her. And that attraction pushed me towards the face of disrespectfulness. But one day, the primaeval man inside me woke up. But I could not ditch her. In trying to hurt her, I got a jolt and bounced backwards. Her eyes had burnt… in anger and hatred.

It was not impossible for me to leave that lively Sonajan within 48 hours of the notice. But I still feel compassion for that tender leaf.

✳ ✳ ✳

Xoti

(SATI)

Come then, let me start telling you Lalita's story this time.

Can you imagine what story this is? Indeed. This is a story and it feels good to tell it if there are people to listen. I am about to tell you the story today that was born as a fairy tale in the Sonajan tea estate which was bereft of modernity. This means this is the story of Sonajan's Lalita and I have told stories about Sonajan earlier too.

Another story of the dream-like Sonajan – a story full of deep emotion and sadness. Another different story of a simple woman who had made the silent experiences of her heart and endless tears to be the assets of her life's trajectory.

A woman, whose name was Lalita. The entire experiences of whose heart had one day been articulated in the crazy torrential new rains of emotions into the unknown. But then that was a long time ago. The clouds of the rainy evening had long since crossed the horizons of consciousness. The articulations that had engulfed both sides of that river also are no longer there. You would only see a descendant of Pandu today – enveloped by the fatigue of the path with anguish-filled eyes, smearing endless exhaustion, a woman broken after having removed numerous problems of the threshold. Her pale lips were the blue witness of her silent trauma.

Naturally, the blue was not that of the blue sky – rather that was the recess of the blue-throated. There was no end to the stories of Sonajan. One after the other, a story waited to express itself in the tea estate that changed form twice every year. That is why I was once again ruminating while looking at the small pebbles and remnants of dust strewn across the pathways of Sonajan. It was evening then. The busy day of the tea estate took rest officially for the night. A flock of birds was flying into the horizon after having finished the day's search towards the shelter, built deep inside the forest.

Wait – let me tell you for a moment why I wish to talk about Lalita. If a beautiful and fresh sunflower bloomed with the divinity of an exclusive garden and it was awaiting its end lying in a neglected street with no one knowing about it and with no compassion from anyone, then wouldn't the latent memory of that flower swing into one's heart?

And it was as if Lalita was one such flower.

The flower that has withered today was once beautiful and fresh. A young labourer blessed by the bounty of nature with a healthy and stout body. It was a body habituated to physical labour with unshrivelled muscular arms and an ample bosom whose beauty could light a fire in the heart of any man. In fact, in the heart of Assistant Manager Suren Choudhury's too.

Yes – that is what I wish to say. Then let me start a bit from the beginning.

You must have heard the name of ex-MP Bhabendra Narayan Choudhury, isn't it? The aforementioned Suren Choudhury was his nephew. Shri Surendra Narayan Choudhury was a student of City College, Calcutta. He got the job of Assistant Manager just after appearing for his BA exams for a second time. The senior Choudhury was then a Congress MP based in Delhi. The tea estate, which the Calcutta Headquarter of the Company based in Assam had sent Suren Choudhury to, was the Sonajan of our story. The Sonajan tea estate, harboured stories of many a darkness and bright history in its bosom and kept staring at the sky.

The Assamese clerks of the tea estate had been quite elated that this elite, proud, temperamental and good-looking young man had been appointed as Manager despite being an Assamese.

"Don't you see that? A dark man also became an ear-scratching Manager of a foreign company. What blood don't the Assamese have?"

"Yes – even the Bor Sahib would not stand a chance in front of Choudhury Sahib's English!"

"Indeed, indeed. So what if he is young, the man is talented. He is of a good lineage too – seems he is from some Zamindar's house. He has handled the entire office even after coming new."

And then there was a discussion by various people on Choudhury Sahib. Let us leave all that.

But then I had started to tell you Lalita's story. A living story of mighty helplessness – as if the grass beneath the feet had become a hooded serpent on the spell of the forest itself. That event had made her, within a moment, quite exotic. That story. That very story.

And now for some preface.

A few people, not quite acquainted with the tea garden way of life, have this notion that money could be made here and life could be enjoyed. In contrast to the four boundaries of the broader society, the freedom of boundless life could not be constrained here. If one could find the sources and research, there could be found unique lakes for boating by restless youth. For a youth, attracted by the excitement of foreign novels and beauteous, arrogant body, it would be irresistible.

And that is what happened in the case of Assistant Manager Choudhury.

He would often see a young labour girl, on his way to inspect work at the tea estate. She would be digging the roots of the tea bushes, removing the vines and creepers and engaging in conversation and laughing with her workmates. Her bright cheeks would turn red and salty sweat would drip down her aquiline nose. While working, sweat would wet portions of the chest area and armpits of the fitted blouse.

There would be the sun on top and, below, would be the tea bushes in columns. There was no shade. It was as if Choudhury Sahib would drink up that beauty…that drug. That labour girl was magical and exotic. The flesh of her bosom would tremble like a pair of ripe papayas in the playfulness of her laughter. And Choudhury's eyes would be arrested in the light of that beauty. He would become listless and the primitive man in the garb of masculinity would wake up. Emboldened, he would take a few steps forward.

Days go by. Choudhury Sahib's steps went further.

The cunning steps of the description-less malefactor were perceived by the simple labourer girl. She turned cautious.

And then one day, there was hell raised. There was pandemonium everywhere. She had landed two slaps on Choudhury Sahib's face. It was a dramatic event. The people were taken aback. Chot sahib vanished in a trice and Lalita kept standing there like a hooded cobra which had received a blow on its back. It was as if poison was dripping down her mouth.

"Don't you have a mother and sister in your house, you scoundrel?"

It was something that had never happened at Sonajan tea garden. Unbelievable! People started talking – some were excited, some had opinions galore, some were scared – wondering what would happen today. It was as if someone had brought hornets into the women's group. Lalita did not say anything more but merely adjusted her clothes. Her eyes were gleaming with rage.

Could people really be that shameless?

The cancer of the twisted taste of elite society was yet to ruin them – they could not digest the uncouth behaviour disguised as harmless fun. She was a simple girl brought up in the routine life of tea gardens: the alluring gift of innocent nature had found expression in the limbs of her entire body. There had been no seraphic dreams woven in her mind – there was no crazed speciality in that life. No complicated thoughts had tainted the simple experience of her open-mindedness. It was that simple – a life made sweet by the conviviality of soil and dust. Yet, if required, that heavenly horizon could steel itself into the promise of thunder that can burn a body to cinders.

Little thoughts and little issues…the laughter, tears and simple mind of the earth enveloped by the limits of the wind…a young girl smeared with the love of soil and sunshine …

And yet, this girl too turned raging one day…

And within a single day, this incident had engulfed Sonajan like the perceptible fire in the crazed winds of Phagun. But no male could express himself in front of the natural eternal rage of a woman. There was no report against her stating that she had insulted the Assistant Manager.

Imbued with a light coffee colour, Sonajan was then busy in the propitiation of a green festival. The restless noise of the factory had turned into an entertaining murmur. There was no smell of raw leaves. Bunches of blossoms were hanging from the branches of the Shirish trees like a pregnant woman. There was a tiredness of dust and afternoon sleep on the roads and like a listless pair of eyes, Sonajan seemed to have retired depressed.

And it was as if in such a moment that Lalita had willingly poured an endless restlessness in the tired body of Sonajan.

Just as I had said – this Sonajan is extraordinary. There is no end to its stories.

It would have been nice if I could have ended whatever I had to say right here. But then, Lalita is alive.

Indeed, she is alive, and that is why I had to write more. And that is because I am about to tell you about her here too.

The Lalita who had planted two slaps on the cheeks of the malefactor Sahib who had set out to ruin a young girl, and who had created an extraordinary tale in Sonajan was today a very common woman with no colour or attraction. If one were to see her now, one would see rhymeless hard prose instead of a piece of poetry – someone who had herself become oblivious to life's struggles. As if a firefly which had gone skywards in search of freedom had flown into a storm and fallen down unconscious in the nearby drain.

I did not set out to write this story enamoured of some lightning beauty which could light up life and youth. A free-spirited bird which had gone out in search of elixir had been given the recess of the earth instead and, having accepted that as God's wish, she held the dreams of the sky in her heart and was passing the days imprisoned in a small cage. I was enraptured by her pride that could tolerate these tortures. This path of life was beset with many an anguish-ridden dust and with the smell of withered *bokul* and *sewali*. This dust and this fragrant divine form had been captured in my heart and that is why I set about giving form to this story.

In a remarkably common house of the tea garden labourers' line settlement could be seen a very common woman. She was about 25 or 26 years old – a face with dishevelled hair, listless eyes and adorable lips. With a taut body covered in a grimy saree, this was none other than Lalita. And you would see a man lying in the darkness of this house counting the minutes to his death. He had pale lips and his skin had wizened.

His hair was dishevelled. The few strands of beard on his chin had become dangly and he was the image of a skeleton.

There were a few gunny bags and a few shreds of a blanket on a cot. There was a packet of bidis under his pillow. Half lit stubs of bidi…matchbox…betel nut peel…the red spit of betel nut. Phlegm and the yellowish vomit streamed down near the headrest. There was a hoard of flies over these and at times, they flew and landed on the man's face and nose. His mouth would fill with invectives directed at this enemy who had flocked to attack him. The man would cough at times and grow tired coughing. It seemed as if his breath would stop and then a stream of blood would come out from his heart along with the phlegm and vomit. The bloody vomit would be thrown into an earthen pot much like some poisonous item was being thrown and the mouth of the pot would be covered with a coconut leaf. The doctor had warned them that the illness in which there was blood with vomit was bad. And these were not to be thrown in the open.

That is why Lalita would dig a pit at the edge of the courtyard and throw all that vomit and blood from the pot into the pit. She would often be late by the time she took care of that man and went out to work. It was no small feat to address the needs of a regular patient. In the end, it would turn into irritation of the caregiver. But Lalita was different. I have already said that a free bird in search of an elixir had got the caverns of the earth instead and, accepting that as God's wish, had been imprisoned in a small cage with the dreams of the sky in her heart. The one who had accepted the dust and grime of the anguished road and accepted these as the fragrance of *bokul* and *sewali* had created heaven in this dust-laden earth.

Hence one fine day when I went and stood in front of a house in the slum line, I saw Lalita passing by me with a shy smile and the weight of the world in her hands. I asked what was all that. She seemed helpless as she replied:

"What to do, Babu? The doctor has forbidden him from having laopani, alcohol, bidi and tobacco but he does not listen. He says he gets more cough if he does not have bidi. He was at it the whole day yesterday. There is no way out. I have one and a half rupees left from my salary and I spent that to bring him some laopani. He had three bowlfuls last night and slept for a while. And after that – oh Babu! – it was all vomit, vomit, vomit! He had no sleep for the rest of the night. And I too could not sleep"

What a pitiful sight.

The doctor had forbidden to have bidi, smoke and alcohol and yet the patient wanted to have it. She could not bear the pitiful plea of her diseased and out-of-work husband. She knew that one should not ignore the doctor's words but how was she to ignore her man's request? The house was running on her salary and yet she had to buy bidi and alcohol for her husband with that fistful of money. Apparently, his cough was subdued when he had bidi. And laopani? How was he to leave something that he had had since birth just because he had the disease?

"Go, please go! Bring me some drink… even if it is a little." He pleaded with her as he wiped the spit dripping off the corners of his mouth and he spat out a mouthful of slimy spit. He wanted her to bring alcohol.

She was at her wit's end. Her heart cried for her thirsty husband facing death. She took a few annas and brought back a handful of bidis with a matchbox and kept these by his bed. He smoked quite a few one after the other and then fell back, listless, on the bed. His lungs were tormented by the smoke in his heart and the infection from his deadly disease.

He would suddenly start coughing. And then he would curl up like a worm on his bed and grow tired from coughing till he expectorated. There would be patches of blood and sometimes he would vomit. His clothes would be smeared with undigested food and some yellowish expectorated substances. She would stumble to him and rub away those liquefied substances. She would cup these in her hands as she picked them from the floor and went outside to throw these in the drain.

On top of all this, she had work from eight o'clock. She had to go to work as soon as the bell tolled. She would come home in the afternoon if she found the time. Else she would reach home in the evening after the bell for the end of the work day. She would come and change her clothes; she would take a bath at the government plant and then bring two pitchers of water home.

I would peek in and see the patient lying listlessly and Lalita hurrying to go to work. She informed me that she would drop all that, clean the house and then take her bath. There was some rice left over from last night. There was no longer any time to cook some hot rice for today. It was time for the bell.

I had said: "It is not suitable to keep such a patient at home. What has the doctor at the hospital said? Why don't you ask the Sahib to keep him there or in Jorhat's Mission?"

She didn't say anything. Surely there was nothing in the storehouse of her mind with which she could reply. Her adorable voluminous lips trembled a bit as she said: "God willing, he will be fine, Babu. The doctor has said to trust in God."

This time, I fell silent – I had no opinion to give. I moved away from the threshold of her house – she might get late to work. I had no right to waste her time. I had gone in search of the mystery of staying alive – I had gone to question what experiences made life beautiful and what was satisfaction. I had returned like a wave which returns on hitting a rocky mountain.

Why had this happened? Why had something like this happened?

I used to question myself, had Lalita wished that the man of her heart would be coughing like this while sleeping or would lie counting the moments to his death while expectorating blood in this dark, happiness-deprived, foul-smelling, anguish-ridden room? Had Lalita ever thought that, after having come back tired from the garden, she would have to dump the vile substances of that disease – clean the vomit, and the pitcher full of bloodied cough and putrid spit in the pit not once or twice but time after time? He would cough, shout and scream invectives at the disease and then plead with her for bidi, tobacco and laopani. No! No! Surely Lalita had not wished for this hellish torture.

Then why had this happened? Why had something like this happened?

Who will say why this happened? But a rhyming poem had become a rhymeless hard prose in the life of the labours of Sonajan estate line – with the anguish of life, its description had itself shrivelled.

A firefly had willingly flown to the open and generous sky in search of freedom – unfortunate! Hit by the storm it had descended and fallen unconscious in a dinghy drain of a dark alley.

And yet, this Lalita too had the free time to dream once. With a plump build, cloud-like soft limbs, bestowed by nature with silky hair, full lips, and alluring eyes, she too had once been beauteous, trembling shyly. Womanhood however had washed over her heart's landscape which had been asleep for a long while, much like Ahalya, stoned and sleeping silently in some forest afar away from any signs of civilization. Her heart was filled with an unknown and incomprehensible emotion.

And perhaps, the deepest recess of her soul had been awakened by the zephyr of many a Phagun. She felt thirsty. With the burning thirst of the traveller trudging across the desert, she noticed a stream in the distance. That oasis, surrounded by the shadows of palms beckoned to her too.

✳ ✳ ✳

There was a huge fight in the Sonajan estate's labour line. One side said: "Our girl has been made to elope" while another side said "Our boy has no bad reputation. This girl is bad. Have you not seen her? She is a purely mystical chimaera. She will shake her body and smile coyly at our young lads."

A young girl and a young boy had become untraceable for one night – Lalita and Rupnath. Without having to look far and wide, they were found in a secluded place nearby. And there both sides had started a Ram-Ravan battle. In the end, the Manager of the garden came to know of the incident. The next day there was a hearing in front of the office. The girl made it clear in her meeting with the Bor Sahib:

"I had eloped of my own free will."

The hearing ended amicably – Rupnath's side came to a settlement regarding ga-dhon[29] and the wedding. Both of them were acknowledged as husband and wife.

Sonajan was calm once more. The morning and evening toll of the garden's bell kept things running as usual. The incident regarding the elopement of a girl named Lalita had given amusement to the estate's employees, their families and homely women, before returning to the usual calm.

---

[29] Bride-price

It was this very Lalita. She was a mystical chimaera… the one who had left her chimaera form and had taken the form of a serpent in the book of the young Manager of the tea estate while he was going to experience the 'pagan' way of life.

Let those things be now.

But what was this that had happened in Lalita's life? Why – why had this happened? Just how many years had it been since they had got married? Their honeymoon had taken place in the middle of leaf plucking in the green tea garden of Sonajan shaded by the *shirish*; in the busy work of spade; in the happy atmosphere of worship and festivities. And then she was on her way to becoming a mother. Her natural beauty had spouted even in the dust and grime of the estate where she had been born and been brought up as a girl. Motherhood had graced her body but the newborn did not like the world. An infant had come but had gone back. Lalita's empty lap had not been filled. But her body had undergone a breakdown when the infant in her womb had been superficially induced to come out.

The doctor examined her and said that it was not easy for her to become a mother. But it was as if misfortunes were waiting to attack her one after the other. She had overcome the grief of not becoming a mother by adorning her body. She would turn up like a frisky butterfly in colourful sarees, blouses, ornaments in her nose and ears and vividly colourful bangles in her hand. Rupnath once more started calling her the mystical chimaera.

The bell tolled at the Sonajan factory. There was the barking of dogs, crowing of cocks and noise of naked boys in the middle of the slum line. And then one day Lalita saw something.

Lalita saw that the disease that Rupnath had been ignoring for a long time had rapidly progressed. He had said earlier that he had pain in his chest; and he had a cough and fever at night quite often. And then one day that man had alcohol and vomited. There was blood mixed in the vomit. He did not have too much alcohol earlier, but later he started having a lot of it. It was not as if she too didn't have a swig or two on happy occasions. But Rupnath was of a different type. Even the gums of his teeth had blackened after having had so many bidis and cigarettes.

The doctor examined the patient. And then…

It has already been said. "God willing it will be okay, Babu. Doctor has said to trust in God."

If anyone went to see Rupnath today, they would see a man lying in the darkness of a room in the slum line of the Sonajan tea estate, counting the moments to his death. A body ready for cremation, sunken eyes and the look of a skeleton. There were a few gunny bags and the shreds of a blanket on his cot. The house was the scene of a living hell…

And they would see a woman. She would be around 25-26 years of age. As if a delicate flower had withered under the tortures of the world. Her name was Lalita. Once a mystical chimaera. She had an attractive body which shook when she laughed. The young boys would be afire. But today, with listless pair of eyes, and deep anguish in her adorable voluminous lips, she is either going out to work or throwing the patient's expectorated spit, phlegm and bloodied vomit in the drain nearby.

The narration of Lalita's story is done: one more story of the Sonajan filled with deep pathos… An extraordinary story of a common woman who had made the deep experiences of her heart and the endless tears the assets of her life's path.

✳ ✳ ✳

XINDHUR XWAD

(THE TASTE OF THE OCEAN)

A little bit further…

Keep coming with me… at least let us see Dr. Dasgupta's palatial building once…

There it is.

Indeed – this is the bungalow of the Chief Medical Officer of our region – Dr. K.M. Dasgupta. Are you surprised? Read that nameplate.

"Dr. K.M. Dasgupta; M.B.B.S; D.T.M.: M.R.C.P. (London)."

Chief Medical Office – Rupajuli Circle. Thirty-eight hospitals fall under its purview. I had already told you some of the names. The entire responsibility of the treatment procedures, medicines, earnings, and actions to take on serious conditions of patients, overseeing all these works and giving due recommendations rest on Doctor Sahib. When it is no longer possible to treat any patient there, that particular patient is shifted to Medical College or the nearby Mission Hospital at the estate's expense.

But then this arrangement had started only now.

There had been a change in perspective amongst the owners and administrative community of the gardens after there had been the creation of a class of labourers who could arrange meetings, and strikes in support of their rights under the supervision of labours – readied right after independence or under the supervision of the pan Indian organization INTUC which had recognized tea employees' associations and tea labourers' association in Assam. But there had been a time when patients, long since lying around in hospitals, had not been healed by the treatment procedure. On the other hand, when the costs of treating a terminally ill patient were suspected to be higher than it was due, then he was not allowed to bear the pains of this world – rather, arrangements were made for his rebirth.

The death of labour in a tea garden was a very common occurrence. His dear ones would wail and cry for a while; then they would take him and bury him in the public cemetery after which on the appointed day they would see 'Howlett' or advance from the Manager for the last rites.

And the garden would continue to run at its natural pace. But…

Oh, just see! I have started speaking of some other topic. You must be bored.

Alright – you have already seen Dr. Dasgupta's bungalow (I will however refer to him as 'Dr. Sahib' from now on because that is how he is known by everyone). You might remember – I had been telling earlier – that this was not his own place. This was only Dr. Dasgupta's designated residence.

In other words, this picturesque bungalow surrounded by green foliage in a deserted area was the official quarters of the Rupajuli Chief Medical Officer.

Have you noticed the wide beautiful green grass? Seasonal flowers of myriad colours and forms? There were colourful vines to keep the portico cool in summer and protect it from the tortures of pre-monsoon dust. In the lawns far off, there were gulmohar, eucalyptus and a few common cacti.

But then this work of art was owing to Dr. Sahib's care. Because there had been an experienced and long since employed gardener who had supervised the garden carefully and owing to whose responsibility, this scene had been created.

But after Dr. Sahib came here, there had been a new avenue of acquisition.

What was that?

A small sapling. A little bed had been created in a secluded corner of the eastern corner of the compound of the Rupajuli Chief Medical Officer Sahib's bungalow and the small sapling had been planted there. It was a small basil plant and now there were a bunch of shrubs there from the seeds that had fallen. And, every day, when the evening skies grew sombre with an inexplicable depth and when the western horizon far way is set ablaze, then – just then – a woman would tiptoe and light an earthen lamp there. And she would leave a prayer there.

It was natural for this scene to create an unusual feeling in this huge bungalow which had two cars, two huge foreign pedigree horses, half a dozen dogs from various nations that created fear, numerous hens and graced with all modern amenities, isn't it?

What to say – Dr. Dasgupta was himself an unusual creation.

Someone had jokingly said that Dr. Sahib consumed alcohol worth Rupees Nine Hundred in a month. He had created a stock equal to any modern bar of any cosmopolitan city in his house by sourcing different coloured and costly liqueurs from different cities of the world including London, Paris and Japan. Whenever he would go out of Assam, he would even smuggle in, if required, any good 'thing' that he could find.

Dr. Sahib often went out of Assam. By 'out of Assam', I do not mean Delhi or Calcutta. He had gone to all the great cities of the world. Dr. Dasgupta was not just a medical practitioner – he was a naturalist and a philanderer.

He had information about wildlife and any curious facts about the sanctuaries of Assam, Kaziranga, Nambor and Manas etc., at his fingertips. He had documentary-like reels shot with his own movie camera on various wildflowers flowering in the foothills, different tribes which were distinctive from an anthropological perspective or various insects and moths. He had a sixty-millimetre projector. He used to do all this whenever he could find the time. The Chief Medical Officer of Rupajuli Dr. Dasgupta was a familiar name in the Information and Publicity Division of the Government of India.

That is why I told you that he was an unusual creation.

Ah! What a beautiful evening!

On this beautiful evening tour, I showed you a picturesque and beautiful house set far away from the general din. I even told you about the owner of this house. You got information about a new person. But how much did you get? Wonder how much I myself was about to tell? It is not possible to give all information about a person ever. Especially when it comes to Dr. Sahib, it is even more impossible.

But a lot of people in the thirty-eight tea estates of this circle circulate strange news about this strange man. As the stories roll off mouths and ears, the stories seem like a piece of stone sliding over a snowed courtyard in winter. It becomes quite difficult to make out what is true and what is false.

"Yesterday, the Doctor Sahib danced the whole night with the memsahibs of this and that garden. The smell of alcohol and cigarettes and the bodies of the dancers mixed together as if it was the Raas-Leela of Shri Krishna and the Gopikas."

"It seems a group of cowherds had climbed the tamarind tree and had looked at the pond behind the bungalow. Doctor Sahib was swimming and frolicking with the college-going daughter of the estate's Punjabi Assistant Manager. When the girl surfaced, those rascal boys saw that she was akin to a child – there was not a single cloth either at her waist or shoulders!"

And many other things. Many!

So many people started rumours – one felt like covering one's ears if they heard these. But how would you gag countless people? Who would raise the questions of truth and falsity?

"What is there to call truth or falsity? Have the ears been sullied?"

But then one thing was true that Doctor Sahib was unmarried. He was around forty years old but he had a beautiful appearance. As if age had challenged him and had been defeated. His body was brimming with the bounty of endless youth.

He used to play tennis and swim regularly. He was an expert in riding and driving. A good portion of his day went into training half a dozen dogs from various countries and playing with them. Even after handling the affairs of thirty-eight hospitals, Doctor Sahib found the time for his playful activities.

This was truly surprising. Who would not be surprised? You need not go far – you can ask any person in this Rupajoli circle and pat will come the reply:

"Doctor Sahib is not a human – he is panacea incarnate. During Hariya's time…"

Was there just one case to cite an example of? There were numerous! Leave alone the cases that he treated…

The labour overseer Saikia had a pampered one – a seven-year-old rascal of a son. He was riding a cycle three double when Saturn squished him – the spokes of the free wheel squashed the toes of his left leg. His left hand also had bent above the elbow so much so that the elbow was indiscernible and the bone too had broken.

Doctor Sahib was on inspection there that day. Just see the fate – the boy who had been frozen as if split into three had been taken to hospital. He examined him and said: "He has a fracture. He has to be taken to Mission."

It was done and two hours later, he took the boy in his car to the Mission Hospital 52 miles away and got him admitted there.

Now that boy studies in high school.

In another estate there was quite an issue – the company issued a notice and made arrangements for three couples to be evicted. They were labours of the estate and had lots of children. One of those couples had a relative who was the water man at Doctor Sahib's bungalow. And that was a connection of connections.

But Doctor Sahib was not required to break his head over such issues and neither did he have any power to do anything. But then I have already told you – he was an unusual man.

Later it was seen that the company retracted the notice.

These are fairy tales – indeed fairy tales. But Doctor Sahib's personality was no fairy tale. Hence the ill said with the conviction of their lives: "If I am not healed by Doctor Sahib's touch, then it is not my fate to be healed."

So many things and so many stories!

It was as if he danced on the waves of such praise and devotion and, yet, how many actually knew him? It was just akin to the blind seeing an elephant.

But then, it was different with Banowari.

Why was it different?

Indeed – that is also a mystery. There can be no solving of this mystery in Rupajoli. How many questioned who exactly Banowari was… how many minds grew curious regarding who Banowari was to Doctor Sahib.

But no one could give an answer and the curiosities were not satiated.

Yet, everybody knew that Banowari was an important living being for Doctor Sahib.

She was a young Saotali girl – aged around 30 or 32. With a visceral full-blooded beautiful body. She dressed like a nurse from the hospital. Her expressive eyes, which were like drops of dew atop banana leaves upon which the sunshine had fallen, could enter one's mind. The tone of her body was like that of a *magur* fish which had just been fished out of the water.

As soon as it was evening, Banowari would change her dress. She would take a bath and then leave her hair open. She would wear a clean white dress and appear to be someone from another world.

After that, maybe, she would look skywards once. There would be the lamps of stars alit in the skies far away. Slowly, Banowari would light an earthen lamp and leave it near the bed of basil.

The huge bungalow would be entirely silent.

Sometimes, when Dr. Dasgupta was not out, he would stand in a corner of the veranda and watch that divine scene. No one knew – away from the crazy din of the civilized world, two drops of tears would flow from the eyes of this unusual man at witnessing this fascinating moment.

Banowari.

Apparently, Doctor Sahib had brought over this girl – once a student at a Missionary school and trained as a nurse – from some organization in Central India. And she made arrangements to fill a great emptiness in the life of Doctor Sahib. He used to give Banowari the same inconveniences with which a child derives value from its mother. He also sought the same behaviour and characteristics from her, like those of the woman of the house, which transformed the floor of a small house into a heaven.

The feeling that the presence of a beautiful women incites in the mind is unparalleled. It was as if Doctor Sahib had found an eternal truth after having roamed about to many places in the world in the company of many women.

He had met quite a few in Rome, Paris or London – heavily overdressed, with rouge and lipstick; the smell of garlic in their breath; with a cigarette in their mouth of their beautiful faces and the experience to pierce through many an appeal with a lilt of their gait; young girls capable of flirting by flaunting their descent or their economic stability; many research scholars or specialists; women who could teach manners in society.., and many others had he met.

But then – where? There was nobody who could fulfil the absence of Banowari.

And that is why she would rush to him as soon as the Chief Medical Office of the Rupajoli Circle Doctor Dasgupta would come home from work. She would kneel in front of him and untie his shoelaces; remove his clothes. And she would take him to the bathroom and bathe him in the hot water basin. As soon as Doctor Sahib returned to the bungalow, his two hands became useless. And Banowari would do everything for him.

There had to be a new flower arrangement on the dining table. She had to be at hand when he was eating. The cook's work was done as soon as the meal ended. His bed had to be made; flies had to be squatted; his body had to be massaged. In fact, he took Banowari's assistance even for grooming his beard.

This unusual man, who was the panacea incarnate for the patients of thirty-eight estates, had his headache cured only at the touch of Banowari's hands. It was her soft essence that calmed his crazed existence. She would run her finger through his hair, massage his head and body and Doctor Sahib would fall asleep.

She would bring down the mosquito net, turn off the lights, close the wooden door and then Banowari would go out from there.

The room in which she slept was at the other end of that huge bungalow.

An old labourer was the guard for her home. He was her guardian. And yet, even all the experience of that old man could not solve the puzzle – what was Banowari to Doctor Sahib?

Who was it that could solve it?

But you know, there was no end to my curiosity in those days. And yet, I had failed. The habit that I had; the joy I derived from digging the grave of someone's mind and bringing out the treasures herein in front of the world had failed miserably. There was no end to my sense of wonder.

I had not told you earlier. Please listen now …

I had met him twice earlier. Doctor Sahib. Once, at his bungalow and the second time by the banks of a small rivulet. Let me tell of the second day first…

There was something wrong with his car and it stopped by that small rivulet. I was out roaming. It was the end of autumn … there were quite a few sailboats like clouds in the blue sky. And this earth was a multi-coloured splendour with the golden rays of the sun falling upon the trees and foliage like a gift.

"Hello." Doctor Sahib was coming towards me.

"Hello. How are you?" I asked.

"I see you all have a lot of time."

"Thank you."

"Okay, you know what. I was thinking something. Assam's natural beauty is so mesmerizing – this beautiful environment can bring about a touch of newness in the minds of people throughout the year. And yet, given the poverty of most of the common people here who engaged in worldly pursuits, and for want of those who can perceive this beauty or who can experience it, the country is at a great loss. The people of Assam should not be poor at least when it comes to their thoughts."

There had been more conversations whose topics would be abrupt, but matter-of-fact.

In the meanwhile, the car was repaired.

But our first meeting was all the more satisfactory for me.

It was dusk and there a lamp had been lit in the bed of basil in front of the huge bungalow.

He greeted me with a copy of Rabindranath Tagore's *Balaka* in his hands. I could make out in the context of our conversation that he was a devout fan of Rabindranath. Doctor Sahib initiated the conversation:

"The essays that you had written in The Assam Tribune and The Statesman on snake bite remedy and local medicine were nice. Indeed, these are quite surprising things. Not just in India, in South East Asia, amongst the Negros specially in Kenya, Tanganayka and other places… Mantras have occupied knowledge and trust in most of these places."

We talked about many things as we had the tea from the table in front of us. The huge radiogram had some Western music on. There was darkness and silence outside. It was as if we had descended into some unknown, unearthly and mysterious seriousness. The smoke of the cigarette took us forward indirectly with the wispy wind. Dr. Dasgupta was a chain smoker.

He was speaking.

I was listening.

I was speaking.

But you know – I cannot help but tell you – I was quite fascinated to see the knowledge that this man of medicine had regarding Rabindranath. He used to tell of the Rabindra

Cultural Associations in Hamburg, Berlin etc. SHILA's Max Mueller and others had sowed the seeds of the eternal banyan of Indian history and culture in Germany's thought processes. And since Rabindranath was the symbol of this history, that is why he had an unchallenged place in Germany (why just Germany; in the whole world).

Dr. Dasgupta told me:

"You know, I often had to hear a complaint in those places – that we Indians were starting to limit Rabindranath and yet this Maharishi had been able to establish himself without revolutionizing the minds of Indians. Maybe you all will say that Rabindranath's birth made India even more glorious but we will always nurture this belief that Rabindranath was a talent."

He had got up in the middle of the discussion and had brought two books – 'Rabindranath as I was told' and 'People and the World.' I saw that he had written both books. He had written the second book on the people and different countries of the world that he had travelled to.

The books did not go back in – I got them with his compliments. He happily signed both and gave them to me.

I had left his bungalow that day fascinated and filled with wonder.

In contrast to all the rumours that I had heard about him, the picture that emerged in my mind's eye was of a beautiful human being with a bright pair of eyes, a well-structured body and well-cultured mannerisms – in the deepest recess of whose mind was bundled a lot of treasures.

So you see – I had told you – that Doctor Sahib was himself an unusual creation?

Let us return once more today. It is dusk.

Who knows – maybe Doctor Sahib was not there in the bungalow today. Surely he was there in some club. Not just that – maybe he was even dancing around having been unable to discard the request of some drunken fair young girl. The waves of the dance would at times breach the brittle shore of decency. The skirts which covered their thighs seemed to want to leave and fly away. In the peak of tiredness and the rhythm of dance, they would try to scratch away the cloth on the chests, waver in search of shelter and open their arms for an embrace. But apparently, there was no maiden in Rupajoli Circle who could tire out Doctor Sahib in dance.

Or he could be in the drawing room. And if he was there, what was he doing there?

He could be reading Rabindranath's poems. Where else could he get the suitable time to get lost in such an intellectual beauty?

Or maybe he had made himself disappear from this well-decorated room and was sipping peg after peg of alcohol? The cook brought in chicken that had been cooked and, seated quietly nearby was Banowari – the carp-coloured young Saotali woman. She was wearing a white dress much like the plumes of a crane – she was healthy and curvy. As if she was some wildflower sought by many. A sculpture, infused with the fragrance of that flower, was sitting beside silently. That sculpture had not noticed the flower or touched it. But it was happy in the thought that this flower was there by its side unbeknownst – its fresh petals would be there for a long time to come. And yet there was no sound from its lips.

Or maybe it could also be that the sad night was slowly descending over the skies far away. In the light of a few scattered stars, a few black-cloud glaciers were floating in that eternal sea. Calm and silent, a man stood alone in the corner of the veranda and wished to search for the taste of that sea. There was a lamp burning below the basil.

No one knew that in this anguished moment, tears were streaming down unstoppably from Dr. Sahib's eyes.

Who knew? Who knew?

Now it is all dark – let us go back.

* * *

Eti Mon Jiya Pokhi

(A HEART-WINNING BIRD)

A group of students in the sixth year of Guwahati University's Anthropology Department were undertaking an educational trip as their field study during the long summer vacation. A compulsory part of their syllabus, this was both a necessary and important aspect. The group would always be under the supervision of a senior doctorate professor.

Animesh and the others had come as part of one such group in 1960. Animesh Dutta. A student in the sixth year of Anthropology.

The field for the tour of Animesh and the others was near Kaziranga. It had been arranged for them to collect data on Social Anthropology related topics, amongst the Gond tribe of the hilly areas of Madhya Pradesh, from an anthropological perspective. There were quite a few human settlements near the gardens in the western region of Golaghat and in their vicinity.

These people had come to Assam to work in the tea gardens. These people had been included as 'tea garden tribe' as per the official procedure of the government. In due course, their numbers increased and whether at the instigation of the tea garden administration or for other characteristic reasons, a few of them went out, occupied official lands and grazing grounds and established colonies there. From a historical perspective, the Gond tribe had a glorious past and they were amongst the best of the ruling people invested with the seed of courage. Even though their illustrious and glorious past had faded over time, their powerful bodies; the beauty of their women who had innocent allure in their eyes; their social coalition; their fearless honesty and their courage which could evade death also, when necessary, and still bear traces of their past identity of yore.

The physical build of the Gonds, their distinctive attire and the characteristic features of their marriage and sexual tribes were attractive and interesting for an anthropological researcher. That is why it had been decided that Animesh and his group would go there this year. The University administration made arrangement in black and white, through government sources, for them to set camp in a garden adjacent to Kaziranga National Park and to stay there.

The Silguri tea estate.

Animesh and his group's lodgings were in the huge bungalow of the Indian Staff Club there. Quite a number of the sahibs, clerks, overseers and in fact even labourers came over to see them. The microscope, blood analysis apparatus, tape recorder, camera, transistors and other instruments created quite a sensation amongst the simple people who led a very common and calm lifestyle.

For the overseer – going to work as per the factory bell, making work entries, making minute entries in huge books, supervising the beating, colouring and steaming of tea leaves amidst the thundering noise of the engine – it was not possible to have the thought that there could be anything to learn about the people they saw regularly in their garden. There had been no opportunity for these people, acquainted only with high school, running around in a limited circle of Gondis and thinking of their livelihood as the primary objective, to learn about a word like 'Anthropology.' Hence, even though they liked talking with the mannered young men and women associated with modern material science and social science, and even though they marvelled at the foreign degree of the professor, nothing that the group said – including their description of how Anthropology was relevant to real life and its importance in knowledge-making – could make an impression on their minds and thought processes.

Alright… be that as it may. As per the plan, the group went ahead with roaming around and data collection. Pushpamala was an associate of Animesh. She was a girl so beautiful one could never get weary. Pusppamala Seleng. Animesh would prepare the questionnaire and Mala would take copious notes. Animesh would take photographs and Pushpamala would participate in the blood group study. Neither of them would be jealous of the talent or research prowess of the other and they would go about their joint work together.

Different people from different strata would come to meet them. Some would come to ask if there was any inconvenience regarding their stay; others would ask what they accomplished today; a few more came to see what these people who had come for their special task wore, how they dressed, how they talked or had fun; and some came simply out of curiosity.

This last group was usually young restless school-going students. Champakoli was in one such group.

Champakoli was the daughter of a tea garden labourer. She was a youngster with a mind made fragrant by one or two blossoms of the spring. She was aged fourteen or fifteen… a beautiful blossom flowering somehow in the secluded forest area somewhere. She would gaze at these representatives of the new age who had come from some city named Guwahati, like a restless deer's simple and happy gaze at vibrant fragrant green grass shimmering in the light of sunshine by some mountain brook.

Pushpamala and the others also took notice. She seemed to be different even amongst the boys and girls seeking an audience. She had a soft, youthful unexplored body whose every beauteous particle seemed to be brimming with the new songs of dawn. She was wearing a pink saree with a green sleeveless blouse. Even though she was not as fair complexioned as a rose petal, she had an attractive brightness in her dark complexion. Her left arm was hidden by the saree while her right arm was naked in a way that could drain a naughty gaze with its promise of fullness.

Animesh too had noticed. And so had the others.

"She is quite a sweet girl," Animesh said to Mala with a smile.

In the end, one day, Pushpamala called her over.

Her name was Champakoli Das and her father's name was Mukundo Das. He was a carpenter in the garden. He was an artificer who made wooden boxes for exporting tea – an artisan class person. She studied at the newly opened Venture School nearby in Class IX.

Champakoli too would ask Pushpamala things. She asked almost all such questions which could prop in the mind of a student studying in a private school of a secluded place. Champakoli had seen the gifts of modern technology – the radio and helicopter. She had heard her teacher describing oxygen and the electric bell in class. She had also seen cheap movies that were love-based or religious-based during the monthly or fortnightly screenings. Hence, it was not as if the winds of newness had not touched Champakoli and the others of her community.

But Anthropology? This whole field was unfamiliar terrain for her. Baideo (she had started addressing Pushpamala as Baideo) used to explain to her and Champakoli tried to understand. A girl studying in the ninth standard of a Venture School had opened the doors of her mind and was letting in the light of the new horizon.

Animesh too started liking her.

Even though he was a student at the University and a representative of modern thinking, there were a lot of open spaces left in his mind for the verdant affection of the damp soil of the Dhansiri. On that soil was heard the dancing sound of anklets of the new season. Animesh did not have any perverted pleasures; there was no meaningless restlessness of the unripe youth's body. The simple beauty of the Champakoli blossom as seen in Champakoli filled Animesh's eyes. She used to call him 'Kaku' – uncle.

Animesh had gone out with her on many days. He had even spent time in her house and talked with her father. The company had built them an ordinary house, but touched by a young girl's many-splendoured mind which had seen the light of modern education, the rooms of the house and the courtyard had an eye-catching environment.

Mukunda was a straight man – he had not had much education. He had not had the opportunity to stay in good company or in an environment of exalted thoughts. For the people whose lives ran as per the sirens of the factory, the water in a puddle trudged by cattle had the depth of the ocean.

He was a craftsman working in the factory of the Siliguri garden. His wife had a company job in the garden itself like ten other women. The elder son was above Champakoli: he could not study much but neither could he secure a company job for himself. He would puff about in shoes and clothes, coat and long pant bought with his father's money and would just roam around. He was the reason for much discontentment in the house. He would watch movies in various gardens along with a group of aimless boys like him; he would tease young girls whenever he could; he would make excuses in order to sit and gamble – these were his activities. But Champakoli turned out to be different. It was as if she was a champa blossom flowering away from the public gaze amidst knee-length grass. With their limited means, she had passed from one class to another to reach the ninth standard.

It was spring – a bud blossomed. Excited by the light of the morning, it was a lovely champa flower. Champakoli. A soft young girl. A beautiful and simple mind. A pair of adorable eyes. No conversations…no words… and yet those full-blooded lips that had an unknown allure. She had not had the opportunities afforded by higher Aryan society. Champakoli knew that the Assamese society had always ostracized the numerous tea garden labourers.

That was the experience of Silguri too. The boys and girls who would sit alongside her in class and those with whom she was friends, would leave school as soon as they were registered as garden people. There was no social contact between boys and girls from households of Assamese or Bengali-speaking clerks or overseers with her house because her identity in the garden was that of 'Mukunda's daughter'. And Mukunda was a labour class person.

To that house, came Animesh.

Once. Twice. Multiple times.

He would come and sit; talk about various things and have betel nut. Mukunda was elated. Her mother was proud. Scared, Champakoli's brother would keep his distance. And Champakoli? Perhaps only God could understand her feelings.

Pushpamala too had come one day after taking due permission from their professor. Even though the other boys had not visited their home, Champakoli would often engage in fun whenever she visited their camp. One of them had named her 'Ratanpur Laxmi.' She would smile coyly and seek protection from Pushpamala Seleng.

And then one day, the excursion party left.

Taking many of them by surprise, Animesh chose to stay back for a few days.

He told his professor: "Sir, this is the first chance I have had to step inside a tea garden of Assam. I have become more interested in knowing about their art and culture."

The professor laughed: "You don't have too many days before the vacation ends."

"I know that, Sir," he pleaded. "I only wish to stay back for a few more days and collect some of their folk songs."

Pushpamala Seleng looked at him with naughty eyes – maybe there had been a bit of unreasonable pride in that look. Someone recited a few lines softly:

"Since a thousand years that I have travelled this path – I have been at peace…"

"Take care – the more the taste in the honey of the wildflower, the more its stickiness…Haha!"

They waved and the vehicle left Silguri garden and went on its way.

"Kaku, you stayed back?"

"Let's go to your house," he held Champakoli's hand. Soothing. Soft. She looked towards him once. There was an air of mistrust in her eyes. Wonder. It was such a wonderful feeling. A common girl from the lower strata of tea gardens. With her walked a much-read young scientist. Healthy and a decent body. A powerful mind. Transparent behaviour. An open mind.

With a simplicity of thought, Champakoli wondered: 'Who was this deity from far? You are far above my reach and yet you are so close to me.'

Mukunda was ready to bear all inconveniences to accommodate his guest. He had hesitated at first. "It would be better if you stay at one of our Babu's houses. We stay in a filthy society – you will be ill at ease."

"Why would I stay out of a society which I have come to learn about? You need not worry please."

This arrangement had been made earlier. Hence, as soon as the vehicle carrying the team had left Silguri, Animesh slowly proceeded towards Champakoli's house with her.

He became a guest for a few days in Champakoli's house.

It was an opportunity for him to garner new life experiences. He tried to learn more about the labourers of the tea tribe; he would roam around the lines of the garden's labourers. The people would stare at him. He would try to enter their mind space and establish a cultural relationship with them. He was Assamese – they were also Assamese. Then it was the duty of the representatives of new thought and new age to start a revolution for a collective experience with them.

At one time, the people of Austric, Dravidian, Negrito, and Tibeto-Burman people bore the flag of Assam. Every legend, river, hill, and community of Assam bore witness to that. Just the other day had come the Ahoms, the Mughals and so many tribes and sub-tribes. They all contributed with a tributary each to the cultural *Bor Luit* in the soils of Assam and they created a huge cultural landscape. Time created a sweet communion.

Was it necessary today to repeat that history?

"Kaku, will you have boiled eggs with tea?"

He was startled. Champakoli had her wet hair high up. She had wrapped a *gamusa* and her *mekhela* was short. The buxom dark flower could be seen a little.

She had shown Animesh everything around: their garrulous society; their groups of women and young girls; groups working in the gardens; the cries of the Sardar who would go around with a turban in his head; the busy overseer; the children with noses dripping, rotten teeth and bloated bellies; the pigs and cocks; the flock of young girls with the betel nut in their hands, the softly combed hair with waves of smiles on their lips. Champakoli gave him an unforgettable introduction to all of these valuable assets of the Silguri garden.

"Kaku, it seems this shop does not have kaptaan cigarettes."

"Damn! It is not kaptan but Capstan."

She had been asking about it in the shop as per his instructions. They had gone out somewhere when he ran out of cigarettes. With mock anger at her inability to pronounce the English word properly, he gave a light thump on her back.

The sun was setting – they were on their way back after having seen a labourer line far away. Champa and her Kaku – Animesh. The intimate shirish, the wide expanse of the tea garden and the silence of this path bereft of people.

The multi-coloured splendour of the evening had climbed the eastern skies step by step as the two of them walked homewards.

Animesh was experiencing the taste of incredible satisfaction even in the limited environment of Silguri garden. He was feeling an inexplicable and yet exalted sort of sweetness. The people had at first been surprised by his behaviour but when they understood that this much-read Babu, in his endeavour to know more about their songs, dance, fun and frolic, wanted to live as one amongst them, then their illiterate minds overflowed with a deep satisfaction of camaraderie.

They danced jhumur at night – a group of young boys and girls set the courtyard of Muknunda's house alive with their songs, dance and the sound of their madol. This arrangement of theirs had been just for Animesh as he had expressed a desire for the jhumur dance of the tea gardens.

A line of madol played in perfect tandem: *jhaa ghij ghij.*

The light of a pale moon in the skies far off. The cover of black and white clouds wisped by here and there…

Dogs were barking – Silguri garden was self-absorbed. A flock of young girls danced to the rhythm of the madol…

"*In the hills and dales,*
The vines flowers in branches
It would be a plight
If torn were these branches …"
In clear voices, they sang and danced.
Jhaa ghij… jhaa ghij…

An open courtyard. A group of people… their hearts and souls were united. The lilt of the songs fascinated Animesh — he smoked a cigarette. As if he too was restless like the group. A group of girls were dancing and singing…

Oh, my affluent… how would I tie you in a tuck?

The madol's sound grew faster and the feet turned flawless with each beat… the minds in that courtyard grew restless.

Jhaa ghij ghij…

"Kaku, do you feel like dancing?"

Champakoli came and stood by his side, touching her body to his. He kept a hand on her shoulder. And it seemed as if she drew closer still…

Oh my affluent… how would I tie you in a tuck?
Jhaa ghij… jhaa ghij… jhaa ghij…
"Kaku…"

He ran his fingers through her hair… his fingers ran down her left arm… like a rotund, smooth apple, the inside of her arm was full and soft… Very slowly, very slowly, he felt like experiencing the softness… As the drape over her shoulder fell off a bit, it covered his hand…

The dancing ended. The singing stopped. The madol fell silent.

The girls sat down on the threshold of Mukunda's house. They talked about various things…

A man had blocked the light of the lamp. For a while. In some inexplicable urge, Champakoli brought up Kaku's fingers and pressed them to her soft cheeks and lips. Animesh grew agitated.

A man from some advanced city far off. A student of Anthropology at the University.

This was Silguri Garden – a small place where the pride of identity could not light one up. more than that, an ignored society… a common house… some uncommon people.

But beyond all marvels, was this little place alive with the compassion of verdant souls. The realizations of an innocent mind.

A mind… a living bird.

A momentary ambrosia: when the bright beam of a momentous light is expressed in the expanses of greater life…

That light brightens the heart. That was the satisfaction of that smallest of moments. The ocean in a drop. There was an indication of that realization in the gaze of a soft, newly young girl.

"Kaku, you will go away…"

"How can I not…"

"It is time for our classes to start. And how many a song and story have I collected from you. How much more could I inconvenience you?"

Animesh lovingly held her cheeks with his hands and turned her face upwards. Champakoli had tears streaming down her eyes. Plop… they fell on his hands.

"What a strange girl! Champa! Champakoli! Why do you cry?"

She hid her face in his chest. Animesh felt weak and drew his face closer to hers. She looked at him again. Her tears had still not dried. Her lips were silent. Two full lips coloured by the colour of youth. They were held together. He embraced her. And, with all the love in his heart, with all his closeness, with all of his feelings, he drew a kiss on her lips.

It was as if his heart and soul calmed at the taste of that nectar.

"Champa, I will never be able to forget you all." She took one of his hands and pressed it against her face, her neck and the lift of her bosom. He sat down on his bed. She sat down on his lap and his fingers grew naughty.

There was no one at home. it was not yet time for work to be over.

She suddenly became conscious.

"Kaku, Baba and all will be home soon. I have to cook."

She went in, he lay down on the bed. His eyes closed with a deep realization: a small boat was moving forward slowly… There was no hurry or restlessness. But the new star of which nebula had created this vast attraction? That it made the ocean itself restless…

What had happened?

The boat was shaking. The ocean had become agitated.

Such honey! There was such honey in Champakoli's lips! His hands still held the fragrance of the touch on her head… and of the oil in her hair. He brought up his hand to his nose – this was not the smell of oil. This was the fragrance of the lotus of life. The fragrance of the lotus of life.

Champakoli was a little flower. She is unwanted. Let her be pure. There was nothing in the sky of his heart. There was no vivid description… neither clouds nor thunder and lightning.

It was as if his mind was the blue of an autumn evening. And in the middle of that a small star – static and anguished.

At this moment, he was not thinking about going to the University. He was not thinking about leaving Silguri. He was not thinking about going out in the evening.

He was not thinking anything.

* * *

DHORMOGHOTOR KARON BISARI

(IN QUEST FOR THE REASON OF THE STRIKE)

As soon as it was evening, the strike-affected garden fell silent. The labourers who had gone on strike felt elated because the reason that they had gone on strike had been successful. The police had arrested the Sahib and taken him to the Police Station from where they would hand him over to the district without cancelling the bail. Sahib had been arrested as per three or four sections. Someone at the peak of excitement shouted as the police van drew away:

"Wow, you son of a gun –how much fun is that!"

The leaders of the workers association also went back to the district from where the paperwork would start.

The police had tied and taken away two other labourers who had helped Sahib.

'Rascals, Traitors.' Some of the hot-blooded ones amongst them hit the ground with their stick. They thundered in front of the police officials themselves: "The son of a gun should be finished, brothers!"

And I was there watching all of this.

I was a paper man. I had to send news to the paper.

I had come myself without taking the news from others. I used to seal my lips, open my eyes and ears and roam around the whole day amidst the fire of the strike. I heard the groups of labourers who were roaming around and shouting; I paid attention to the opinions of the leaders of the strike; I went to the Sahib's bungalow; I looked at the faces of the accused and the complainants; I heard their interrogation and I heard the responses of both sides.

The day ended – it was as if the police had come and thrown water on the fire that had been burning wildly. The garden was silent.

But – I don't quite know why – I did not feel like leaving. I stayed back. This was not the me that sent news to the newspaper – this was the me that liked to open the hidden and mysterious doors of the heart and peek in.

I used to roam around in the labour lines. They knew me, I was a paper man. Safe. No one viewed me suspiciously and that is why I used to roam around Gogoi Sahib's tea estate freely. Now the men were masticating on the day's events in the verandas of the shops. The women had to enter the kitchens. They had not dwelt on this matter any less than the others had the whole day.

The sounds of the madol wafted in from a corner of the line through the fingers of those who did not like to enter into the winds of any revolt or those who were cowardly or those who were simply bohemian...

Jhaa ghij ghij jaa...

I proceeded along the line towards the house of the president of the Tea Association. I wanted to meet him one last time. If I could, I would meet Radha too. And would tell her that she was human and hence she ought to live with the dignity of human beings.

She had probably been overwhelmed by this huge storm today and then become calm. And she was possibly thinking what kind of a resolution was this to the three-year-old drama.

Gogoi Sahib was possibly on his way to Golaghat. 'Non-bailable warrant of arrest on the charge of wrongful confinement, physical assault with injury; guilty caught red-handed. Persuasion, illicit contact with woman and molestation' – the officials of the association had given these too. The police Sahib however said that this won't stick 'for want of proof – her private parts are long accustomed to physical/ sexual contact'. OK – these would work. For some, insult was injury. There had been quite a lot that had transpired already.

The water man in Gogoi Sahib's bungalow had blurted right on the face of the Huzoor:

"We do not understand all this – we get ashamed. They would not have kids and yet enjoy. There would be no clothes on Radha's body, neither on Sahib's… Tsk! Tsk! Tsk!"

Gopal was now hospitalized. His body had been torn apart – sacrificed to uncontrolled rage.

Gogoi Sahib had shown three applications given to Manager. A group of gamblers had been created in the garden. Their ring leader was purportedly Gopal. He used to do sulai[30] and alcohol business too on the sly. About one and half years ago he had de-registered at the garden in the hope of getting the six hundred and fifty rupees of his provident fund. Number 1 troublemaker. This Gopal was one of the forerunners when it came to the increase of intoxication amongst the labourers; opening the path to losing everything through gambling; hooliganism at the Sunday market or local festivals; assaults and all other kinds of unrest. The assistance for all this was a gang of fans who had been initiated by him. The place of instruction for them was the cheap 'Jassosi Fighting Picture' – the mobile companies would screen such movies at low prices and show them in various gardens.

Radha said: "Ok. Let all that be."

---

[30] Local liqueur

Gopal said nothing as he was not in a state to say anything. His body spoke for itself. In the meanwhile, the estate doctor had administered lakhs of units of penicillin.

So said the officials of the Association.

Gogoi Sahib was wrapped in the long anguish of his self-interest.

The reporter was saying: "We have plenty of documentary proof. Gogoi Sahib wished to incapacitate the Trade Union which had formed in the estate. He used to torture the workers; use hired goons for assault and drive them away from the estate. He would deprive them of their due and used to keep a notorious group satisfied in order to trap people in legal matters and prove them guilty."

"You will be surprised to hear, Sir, whenever we used to come from the district office for organizational work, he would inebriate a few labourers and release them amongst us and we had to flee for our lives."

"But what is the relation of all these to today's incident?" the police officer asked – his eyes on the fish like Arjun's[31].

"There is an important relation – it is part of the whole."

"Fine, tell."

"Today's victim Gopal is a member or our association. He used to work as per our plan and instruction."

"*Including gambling?*" the police officer wanted to create some amusement apparently.

"Please, Sir!" the Association's official surely irritated.

But there were witnesses. There were quite a few people in Gogoi Sahib's estate who openly said that Gopal was not

---

[31] An allusion, perhaps, to Arjun who was one of the five Pandavas in the epic Mahabharata. He had to do the 'Matsya Vedha' and pierce the eye of a rotating fish by seeing its reflection in water in order to win the hand of Princess Draupadi. It required great skill and single-minded focus.

engaged in only constructive activities but that he was attracted also to some dishonest activities.

Each side tried to establish the story from their own perspective. The truth would transpire only if the entire episode was narrated in detail.

When Gogoi Sahib went out to work at the crack of dawn dressed in birthday clothes, Radha was still asleep on the soft bed with the fatigue of a night of celebration. The lids of her eyes opened slowly and, stretching lazily, she got out of bed. The door was closed and there were thick curtains over the windows.

Radha knew nothing could be seen from outside and hence she got up naked from the bed and went near the rack. The nylon saree and blouse were hanging on it since last night.

"Hey there, *Memsahib* – you are up?" the watchman at the bungalow called out on seeing her. She too used to joke with him. She asked for hot water to take a bath – she entered the bathroom and took a bath. There was a shower bath and hot water basin. In the afternoons, the Sahib and Radha would often bathe together.

Each inch of Radha's body was powdered; contraceptive ointment smeared in the required region; the excitement caused by foreign liqueur and then the night-long exertions that happened with the help of all these.

A stream of salty sweat, filled with the smell of men and women, would flow through each and every strand of body hair of each organ on Radha's buxom body. There would be the stickiness of grime in its contours –her body was fleshy and hence the contours too had depth.

This ethereal beauty, between whose extended neckline and smooth thighs was held captive this aged man's mind; whose sweat, hidden in the corners of the svelte body, activated at the base of the sweat glands, smelled in the humidity – the smell of rotten onions – which would drive Gogoi Sahib crazy.

This ageing manager – Gogoi Sahib – was the consumer of all the assets of this twenty-five-year-old body. Gogoi Sahib was slowly moving towards his mid-forties. Everybody in the garden knew that Radha – who had fought and left her husband's side – did not have to go to work like ten other women labourers. She worked at the bungalow.

Gogoi Sahib's family stayed at their own home in the far-off city. The children needed to keep their studies right – if people did not stay in their own homes, it fell to disuse. Gogoi Sahib's elder daughter was apparently of marriageable age and his elder son had matured – he was studying M.A. in Guwahati.

In the garden, Gogoi Sahib stayed alone.

The bungalow watchman, orderly and cook – these were the employees at Bar Sahib's bungalow. For three years now, a young girl of the garden had been arranged to do work required indoors.

Her name was Radha. After having had some fight, she had left her husband's home. then she had just crossed the threshold of twenty years – such kind of women were hollow in nature. If a mind that had experienced the taste of enjoying the body gets the freedom of breaking out of the moralistic cage of the husband's home, then such a young woman naturally becomes inclined towards promiscuity. The same was the case with Radha. She kept looking out for bumblebees in search of honey. But one thing was for sure: a young woman who gives up the flower of her youth to be sucked expects material things in return. These could be expensive dresses, gold ornaments or the attainment of relaxation and luxury. Till the poisonous critter of the mind does not die, such a voracious woman does not wish to enter the nuisances of bringing up children or taking the responsibility of a household with its attendant rules and regulations.

One day, as per the instructions of the woman overseer of the garden, she came to the bungalow. She was entrusted with the responsibility of sweeping, mopping, bed-making and other tasks.

Bor Sahib's bungalow was a huge one. The main person was Gogoi Sahib. No other family member stayed there. The watchman, orderly and the cook ran the household. Radha had her own free pace and endless time – there was too less work but there was the need for attention. At any moment, she had to keep whatever Sahib needed within his reach. Whatever was needed – clothes, bed, work-apparel, shoes, socks, walking stick, hat – had to be handed at the right time.

One fine day, Sahib started joking around with her. Bor Sahib used to have fun with Radha.

Fun slowly turned to attraction. Absolute freedom and sovereign power laid out a golden carpet in Gogoi Sahib's colourful palace. New dresses adorned Radha and new postures took shape in her body. The insolent courage of disobeying the other people in the bungalow took birth in her heart. And then, one day, they all came to know that Radha was perhaps was sleeping together with Bor Sahib on the same bed.

Gopal's advent was around this time.

Gopal was a labour of this garden. He was an artisan at the factory.

Before Radha had come to the bungalow, she had been working at the factory. Gopal felt like marrying her when he saw her. Actually, Gopal had married at the age of about sixteen but their married life had never been stable. His wife too was not too old and unfortunately her first baby had been born prematurely. Since then she grew sickly. Having been bleeding for a long while, the girl became withered and pale like some sapling dried out in the sun. The estate doctor could not treat any patient like that as a result of which she slowly moved towards death. Till the moment of her death, that withering vine had to regularly endure the tortures of that Gopal's then brimming with youth. It need not be said that Gopal's tortures, lack of nutritious food and without the right treatment, the woman died silently one day. The family, considering that to be absolutely natural and the will of fate, felt no particular sadness.

Gopal was now alone. One of two birds had got lost and the other, being freed of the chains of conjoined life, tried to fly to the skies.

It was not as if Gopal had any sense of responsibility towards his home. Everyone earns in a family of tea garden labourers – at least till the time they were engaged in work, they were not dependant on anyone. With the excuse of the elderly in the family keeping their finances in order, a free-minded youth like Gopal could get away his whole life without getting into the nuisances of running a household.

Gopal also did likewise. He turned wild. His alcohol intake increased and he poured his life into gambling. The number of his friends increased as days passed and he stepped into so-called modernity. He acquired experience in developing taste in clothes and appurtenances by watching movies screened in the gardens. With money from gambling came shoes and socks; came watch; came goggles and came cycle. In the words of the clerks and overseer of the garden, Gopal became a 'Babu'.

Even though the officials of the Association tried to tilt the story in favour of Gopal, the curious police official took note of a few things from Radha: first, even though she was not amused, every time he met her, Gopal would ridiculously say "Radha, this time it is you I will marry." One more thing, Gopal would gamble and then create a ruckus at times. But she truly did not know that Gopal had become highly drunk yesterday and had made plans to steal her away to some place. And, she did not say anything in addition to the work-related things of the garden concerning Gogoi Sahib.

The analysis of a few important things remained unclear: example, how was Gopal, who had been held captive in the bungalow since last night, been discovered? Why had Gogoi Sahib, like powerful kings and zamindars, employed hired hands to denude Gopal and given him such merciless punishment? Who had made the incident public within two hours of Gogoi Sahib being in the office? How had the officials of the Workers' Association suddenly appeared on the scene? How had a strike been organized within three hours in the garden after having made this incident the reason for revolt?

A volcano had erupted… smoke… ash… earthquake…

Shouts, screams, din… the yelling of the striking labourers…

Innocent workers cowered…the women were terrified.

Hordes of people went and gheraoed[32] Manager Sahib's house.

"We want justice. We want justice."

Gogoi Sahib was trapped in his house. Alone.

The watchman, orderly, cook, waterman and other workers of the bungalow abandoned their Huzur and in fact, they joined the opposing team and stood against the Manager.

The officials of the Associated were shouting and explaining to the public: "Brothers and friends, mothers and sisters! Calm down! We have called up the Bor Sahib of the district. They will be here soon. There is no fear. Long live, labourer brothers!"

---

[32] Surrounded – a typical tactic of agitation

"Long live!" 1500 labourers screamed in unison. What events had occurred in the course of one day!

It was evening now, it was as if the war zone was now calm. The police van had gone away. The officials of the Association had gone to the district office. The manager of the estate, Gogoi Sahib, and a few people who were like his right hand had been arrested.

There would be a case. Witnesses would have to go and present themselves in court. All that would come later.

I was pondering over things and walking through the lines of the labour colony.

As a journalist, my job of collecting news had ended. An urgent and an important event had been 'covered'.

But the storyteller in me was still not satisfied. And thus, even though I was tired in body, I dragged it to Radha. If possible, I would take someone familiar with me. If possible, I wanted to ask Radha a few things and clear the suspicions in my mind. If possible, I wanted to help modern science by making the hidden chapter of a man's life come to light. I wanted to ask Radha and see: why did she like this life of chasing mirages? Did she wish to keep flying till the time she had the wings of youth on her body? Didn't she dream of a child? Didn't she wish for the sweet environment of a calm home? Why had she preferred to make these the contents of her life's path – a manager, an ageing man, the excitement of foreign liqueur, the powder that covered her body, contraceptive, the sleepless disgusting nights in which the denuded vine of the body surrendered?

I was pondering over all this and going on.

Many things peeped into my mind – would I get any answers? Would she give answers to the questions I had? Maybe, she would be in a state to give any answers today. Then I would not be able to ask her many other things.

I would not be able to ask: had she got to know from the watchman at the bungalow about the excessive thrashing of Gopal at night and, like a crazed woman, had she gone out to the line and informed everyone?

I would not be able to ask: why had she called the officials of the Association to the bungalow after having seen their jeep? Was it because of the tortures inflicted on a man till he was half dead and then imprisoned? Or was it because the man was Gopal?

I would not be able to ask: from where had she drawn the courage to say all that she did in front of the Manager?

Maybe I would not be able to ask: if she had felt pain in the core of her heart on seeing such torture inflicted upon Gopal.

Still, let me go and meet Radha once. I wanted to see up close and personal, the outer form of that body filled with wild excitement. I wanted to try and feel the heat in her heart.

That is why I was going.

Silence descended on the labour lines. A dog was standing at someone's threshold and barking. Snippets of conversation and waves of broken laughter wafted in from afar. This was the basti-line of a strike-affected tea garden. Darkness was descending now.

I was slowly making my way towards the house of the President of the Association.

My quest was still on…

* * *

www.ingramcontent.com/pod-product-compliance
Lightning Source LLC
Chambersburg PA
CBHW022012150726
47990CB00002B/630